About the Author

A. G. Clayton was born in England. He experienced a happy but peripatetic childhood. Having failed to get into art school he worked as a cinema projectionist, trainee land surveyor, packer, cleaner and cutter, all interspersed with salutary periods of unemployment. He passes the time watching silent films and reading.

The Burial Party

A.G. Clayton

The Burial Party

Olympia Publishers
London

www.olympiapublishers.com
OLYMPIA PAPERBACK EDITION

A CIP catalogue record for this title is
available from the British Library.

ISBN: 978-1-80074-928-3

First Published in 2023

Olympia Publishers
Tallis House
2 Tallis Street
London
EC4Y 0AB

Printed in Great Britain

The Burial Party
Part One

Chapter 1

A hefty shove in the back sent me down a flight of wooden steps onto a hard dirt floor. A door closed, a key turned, and I was engulfed in semi-darkness and silence. After a few moments, I struggled to my feet and let my eyes get used to the gloom. It wasn't a very large basement room with stone walls and two small windows set high up at ground level. The last of the daylight was almost gone and I looked around. A set of shelves off to one side contained glass jars and bottles and there was a pile of wood kindling in one corner. A smell of rotten apples hung in the dank air.

A trickle of blood from my lip tasted salty and warm, no doubt the result of me hitting the floor. I made my way across to one of the windows, reached up and tried to open it, but it was stuck fast, as was the other. But the second one had a small crack in one of the tiny panes of glass. I instinctively reached for the penknife in my jacket pocket but was reminded that my captor had searched me and relieved me of all personal belongings, which were not many — some loose change, a return train ticket, a newspaper, the front door key to the house on the hill — as well as the penknife.

I searched around on the shelf and found an old rusty nail, and wielding it as carefully and quietly as I could, managed to break the glass and let the cold night air in. With the fresh air came the distant sound of a stream — I recalled the one I had crossed earlier that day — also the distant sound of leaves rustling in the breeze. The window was dirty but just visible in the distance was the black shape of woodland against a dark grey sky.

I was exhausted and slumped down, back against the stone wall, my aching legs stretched out. And I was hungry. I hadn't eaten since bread and cheese at the station buffet that morning. *Better not dwell on that,* I thought. *You've been hungry before.* In the trenches it was often days before relief brought up lukewarm tea, bread and margarine. The memory brought on a shiver, or was it the cold night air?

I scrabbled around and eventually came across a couple of hessian sacks, one of which I sunk my legs into; the other I wrapped around my shoulders, but they brought little warmth or comfort. I tried to get my befuddled mind to consider the more immediate problem of what was going to happen next. My captor hadn't believed me when I had lied that I was lost and had strayed onto the property by error. *But why lock me up as if I were a common criminal?* I thought. *Why not summon the local police and have shot of me? Or did they know who I was and what had brought me to Huntingdonshire and Hopeswell Hall?*

Better to get some sleep, I told myself, and face the morning afresh. Before I drifted off, my thoughts turned to Edith. Was she missing "her William"; did she find the note I'd left? Of course she did, it was propped up against the teapot on the kitchen table. But what, in her frail state of mind, did she make of it?

'I am going away for a few days and will get in touch soon...' No doubt her first thought would be the same as ever it was, would I return? With her anxious face in my mind's eye, I fell into a fitful sleep.

I awoke to the sound of a key turning and a door opening. The clank of metal on wood and the door closed and the key turned. A dim morning light came through the windows and revealed the cellar, my 'prison' for the night. I discarded my coverings and climbed the wooden steps. At the top was a tin tray with a hunk of bread and a mug of tea. I ate and drank greedily as I viewed the grounds through the window. A parkland stretched away to densely wooded trees. A gravel drive wound its way off to the left; to the right, the land sloped away into a hazy blue mist, but I thought I could just make out the glistening surface of a lake. Clearly, I was incarcerated at the back of the house. The family vault, which I had been examining when apprehended, must be around the side overlooking the land that sloped to the lake.

I wiped the glass as best I could and tried to get a reflection of myself in the window. The blurred image revealed a gaunt face, a stubbly chin, unkempt dark hair. With my creased jacket and trousers, frayed shirt collar and cuffs and scuffed shoes I looked the typical vagrant, on the tramp looking for work, which was exactly the impression I had hoped to convey. The clothes were 'his' old work clothes I had come upon whilst rummaging in the garden shed. I had dressed early that morning while Edith was still asleep, carefully written the note, then quietly left the house and within an hour I was boarding a train at King's Cross. As it sped north, I occupied my mind with who I was going to be for the next few days. I had deliberately left any identification papers behind thereby conferring on me official 'tramp' status. Should I adopt a new alias or continue with my present one? After much thought, and to avoid any further confusion, I decided to stick with William Perkins. He had served me pretty well over the past months.

I changed trains at Cambridge and a local train deposited me at the small village station of Hopeswell a few hours later. I strolled down the lane, past the village shop and the church, and entered the local inn. The landlord replied to my enquiry as he drew a pint of ale and passed it across the bar.

'Not much work around 'ere now, and you've missed the 'arvest.'

'What about up at the big house?'

'The hall? They've had the same gardener and gamekeeper for nigh on—'

'Old Gabriel's been shooting poachers up there for the last twenty years,' interrupted one of the locals.

'Still, I'll give them a go. You never know your luck,' I ventured.

With the landlord's directions clear in my mind, I finished my pint and set off. An hour later I came to the main gates of Hopeswell Hall. On the brick gatepost, partially concealed by ivy, was the familiar plaque bearing the family crest. The house wasn't visible from the road, just a gravel and dirt track that made its way through an avenue of trees and tall bushes. I walked on and about twenty minutes later, climbed over a high stone wall and dropped onto the domain of the Courtney-Allyns. A thicket of oak and beech trees gave me good cover but I was soon made aware of the risks connected to my enterprise when I almost stepped onto a snare half-hidden under a pile of leaves. A few minutes later, the trees thinned out and I was confronted with a vast expanse of parkland. A stream flowed down to a lake and just beyond was the house, a large grey structure cluttered with balconies, gables, chimney stacks and turrets. Off to the side of the house was a cluster of outbuildings, alongside of which was parked the large black car. Beyond, amidst a clump of trees, was a small cemetery with a vault, built of what looked like marble, and where I hoped I would find what I was looking for.

By my reckoning it was the middle of the afternoon. Only a few hours until darkness descended. I withdrew into the woods, found a well-hidden, uncomfortable tree stump and fell into an uneasy sleep.

At dusk I stirred and made my way to the edge of the wood and looked out at the expanse of land between me and my goal. There was a stillness in the air. The sky was purple streaked with pink. The stream purled past me down towards the distant lake and I could see the green reeds moving with the flow beneath the sparkling surface. A calm came over me and I hesitated before stepping across. Was this what 'Englishness' felt like? And I wondered, if it was, did the people who occupied the large house beyond have similar feelings? I recalled a similar emotion from some years before. Celia and I had gone to a concert at the town hall. It wasn't out of a love for classical music, more a place to go out of the rain and hold hands and be together. One of the pieces was by an English composer, I couldn't recall his name, but its gentle flowing rhythms and melancholic mood summoned up the same feelings as I now experienced. I remember my disappointment that Celia didn't feel the same way; she preferred, she said, going to the cinema.

I skirted the edge of the wood for as long as I could before crossing the stream and making my way down, across the open ground, towards the family vault. All was peaceful, just the sound of birds returning to roost. As I approached the cemetery I noticed a few other burial plots surrounding the main vault. Overshadowing them all was a giant copper beech tree and I hid behind the trunk. My insides turned over as I considered my next move. The wind got up and brought a few gusts containing rain and my mind went back to that day in France and the rain and the mud and the field of corpses… it seemed that death was not going to loosen its grip on me just yet.

Cautiously I stepped forward, and a few yards from the entrance to the tomb, a sound, familiar to me from my time in the trenches, that of a gun cocking, brought me to a sudden stop. I turned to face a man who, from his attire, was clearly the gamekeeper. He had both barrels of his shotgun pointing at my head. A large growling dog was by his side, ready to pounce.

'I've had my eye on you for the last half hour,' he said. 'What do you want here? This is private property.'

I stammered out the story I had concocted, but to no avail. He got me to empty my pockets and then motioned me towards the rear of the house and the basement room where I was now confined.

Fortified by the meagre breakfast provided, I considered that my situation wasn't as serious as it had seemed the night before and that my jailers couldn't be all that bad. Soon matters would be cleared up and they would release me, if only as a vagrant, to the local police. Even though I hadn't succeeded in my undertaking, I was confident that, once free again, I could somehow continue with it.

It was another two or three hours before the door opened and two men descended the steps. The gamekeeper carried his shotgun under his arm. He was a tall, dark-haired man with a moustache, his skin weathered from the outdoors. He was wearing a tweed outfit with leather patches and leather boots, the same clothes he had been wearing when he apprehended me. The other man was about the same age as me, ginger-haired, pale skinned, and had an air of the indoor life; he was chubby around the waist, his movements were ponderous and his voice languorous and high-pitched. He wore a lounge suit, cravat and patent leather shoes as if he'd only just left a society dinner or the gaming table.

'I caught him nosing around the family vault, sir,' said the gamekeeper.

The younger man, obviously finding the surroundings distasteful, looked his prisoner up and down perfunctorily, turned and climbed back up the steps.

'Bring him along, Roberts.'

A few minutes later, after tramping along various narrow corridors, we were in a small oval-shaped room with two doors — one each at either end — and no windows. The only light came from a single bulb hanging from the ceiling. Sporting prints lined the walls, walking boots and shoes were scattered around the stone floor and a couple of foxhounds sniffed me over before being ushered out. Roberts still had his shotgun aimed towards me as he stood at the door we had entered by. The younger man took a silver cigarette case from his pocket and lit up.

I thought it worth trying the same tale I had given to Roberts and assumed a naive expression to go with my explanation. The younger man listened indifferently as he puffed on his cigarette.

'Sit down, why don't you,' was all he said.

I sat on a wooden chest, my back against the wall.

'And what was your interest in our family vault?'

'Nothing... just interested. Like I said, I was lost,' I replied. The younger man's offhand manner led me to believe that my story was not taken seriously.

'My father is the local magistrate. He will be interested in your explanation.'

'Then you've sent for the police,' I ventured, hopefully. There was an anxious exchange of looks between my captors.

'All in good time, all in good time.' He stubbed out his cigarette on the floor. 'Roberts, keep an eye on our guest until

Father appears.'

'But I've got my traps to inspect, sir.'

'Very well. Then return him to the cellar.' He spun around and left the room.

Roberts motioned with the barrel of his gun and I was returned to the cellar for the rest of the day. A tankard of ale accompanied another slice of bread and piece of cheese a few hours later but it wasn't until the evening came on that I was led up to a different part of the house.

As Roberts and I entered, the young man got up from the large round table in the centre of the room where he had been playing a game of cards. He poured himself a glass of whisky from the decanter on the table. Another man stood motionless by the fireplace, his back to the room.

Long velvet drapes were drawn against the darkening sky. Glass-fronted cases lined two of the walls and contained books that had the air of never having been taken out and read. A dull portrait in oil, presumably of an ancestral forebear, hung on the wall above the fireplace. A dusty chandelier hung from the ceiling, but the only light came from two candles, one on the mantelpiece, one on the table. Gloom seemed to be the ambience favoured by the residents of this place, as if they were afraid of the light.

After a few moments, the figure at the fireplace turned and fixed his eyes on me. I recognised him at once but tried to conceal my surprise. I hadn't seen him since that time in France but even without the uniform, his military bearing was unmistakable. The moustache, the hard-set chin, the cold grey eyes were the same. Now, though, on home territory there was a superior air, a self-satisfied attitude, a certainty that came with his position. No self-doubt, no equivocation. He walked towards me, slowly, deliberately, but stopped at a distance that, for him, suited our obvious differences in class.

'Roberts here tells me you were travelling north looking for work, lost your way and entered the estate by accident.' This question directed ironically at me. It was then I noticed on the table my penknife, some coins, a key, a ticket and a folded page of newspaper — I'd forgotten that. He picked up the railway ticket and held it out. 'A man looking for work doesn't buy a return ticket to London.'

A nervous smile appeared on my face.

'Do you think this matter laughable?'

I could feel the presence of the gamekeeper behind me, shotgun in hand. There was an atmosphere of menace about the way they regarded me, as if the trial was over and sentencing was due, but before I could offer an explanation...

'Well, Rollo... what do you make of him?' The older man addressed his son.

'A bastard, sir, and no mistake,' replied Rollo, eager to please with the right answer.

'Do you have a name?' the older man continued. I hesitated for a moment.

'William Perkins.'

'Sir. You should address me as sir.' I ignored this request but a dig in the back from Roberts' gun changed my mind.

'Sir,' I mumbled.

'And do you know where you are?'

'Er, I think somewhere south of Lincoln, sir.'

He picked up the candle from the table and held it up to my face.

'Your face is vaguely familiar. I feel that we may have met. Perhaps in France. Did you serve?'

'Yes, sir. The Sixth Sussex Regiment. I fought at Arras and Ypres.'

There was a considered reaction to everything I said, as if I were in front of a jury of my peers.

'He's a liar, if you ask me, Father,' blurted out Rollo, filling up his glass and taking another drink. But the older man ignored the outburst.

'I am Baron Courtney-Allyn. Hopeswell Hall is the family seat. It has belonged to the Courtney-Allyn family since 1348. For six miles around, this is my land. We are second cousins, by marriage, to the present monarch. When I die all this will pass to my son, Roland, and when he dies it will pass... and so on and so forth.' This was stated with a hint of pride but more as a matter of unassailable fact. I noticed a tinge of regret in his voice at the mention of his son. I tried to assume an air of ignorance although I had learnt a bit about the family. If he had intended to impress me, he had failed.

A silence descended on the room. Perhaps, I thought, I should press home my story about accidentally losing my way on 'his land', but before I could...

'Some time ago, a soldier on a working party near Cambrai, disappeared. He was posted as, "absent without leave". He was due to go before the firing squad for desertion but because of an oversight by the officer on duty that day he was selected to go on a burial detail. Private Edward Burne of the 4th Middlesex Light Infantry was his name.' He peered at me as if to discern any change in my demeanour.

After a moment I replied, 'Like I said, my name is William Perkins.'

'More lies, Father,' said Rollo, leaning aggressively across the table. His glassy eyes betrayed a day of steady drinking.

'It is believed that Private Edward Burne made his way to England where he is still absent without leave,' continued the Baron.

With great difficulty I maintained a bemused expression and repeated my fictitious tale of being an ex-soldier looking for work, who had gone astray. Another long silence followed. I thought I perceived a hint of doubt enter my interrogator's mind.

'What did you do with your uniform?' He suddenly flung at me, hoping, no doubt to catch me out.

'Traded it in for civvies when I was demobbed.'

He turned back to the fireplace. 'I will give you until tomorrow to think things over. Take him back to the cellar, Roberts.'

As I was prodded towards the door by both barrels, a high-pitched voice rang out.

'Ask him about the woman.'

'Yes, thank you, Rollo. I was forgetting that.'

There was no hiding my shock at the mention of Edith. I assumed that she was the woman referred to. In my panic I was tongue-tied, a hot sweat broke out over my body. The faintest of smiles crossed the Baron's face, accompanied by a smirk of satisfaction on Rollo's. 'Now we have him, Fa—'

A sudden decisive hand movement from his father silenced him. 'You see, Edward Burne, we know all about you.'

I tried to regain some sort of composure and after a few moments said, 'Where is she? Is she here?'

'Perhaps, if you told your story… if you confessed, we might consider her situation more favourably… as well as your own.'

The night was long and cold. I huddled in a corner, covered by the hessian sacks. There was no sleep for me as I considered my plight, and more importantly, Edith's. There was no getting away from the fact that although, primarily, she had entered my life at a time when I most needed help, the few months we spent together became more than just a convenient point in time. Despite her fragile condition she had provided unquestioning friendship and support, and warmth. I blamed myself for involving her in my problems; after all, she had enough of her own to deal with.

It was obvious to me that continuing with my 'gone astray' narrative wasn't going to work any longer. The Baron had said, 'we know all about you, Edward Burne,', and with a heavy heart, I considered how much they knew. Was he just doing his duty as a magistrate and arresting an escaped soldier? Or, more worryingly, did they know what I had thought I had stumbled upon, and was that why they had me imprisoned here? The thought filled me with dread. The anxieties built up in my mind until I was no longer able to think clearly and I went into a troubled half-sleeping, half-conscious state… and slowly, inexorably, the circumstances that led to my present situation began to materialise before me…

Chapter 2

We didn't shake hands. It would have been futile, as if by some miracle we were going to meet again. Just a brief nod from Evans before he was led away. I couldn't restrain a smirk, a reaction to tense situations that had developed from over three years in the trenches.

'You'll be laughing on the other side of your face this time tomorrow morning,' yelled Sergeant Major Perry from across the hut. I listened to the disappearing clump of boots as Evans was led away between two guards, then moved across to the window and stared out at the bleak, flat, wintry landscape.

Perfect weather for the occasion, I thought. A crow landed on the ground just beyond the wire fence and started pecking at something in the mud. Another joined it, cawing encouragement.

'Bloody scavengers, they always know when it's someone's time,' observed Perry before he too marched away to join the firing squad.

It was a full ten minutes before the distant dull commands and then the volley of rifle shots echoed across the camp. I turned away and my lips curled in disgust.

'What you up for?' asked Groves, his freckled uncaring face grinning from beneath a shock of ginger hair.

'Same as Evans,' I replied.

A disinterested 'Oh' was all the youngster could muster and he went back to cleaning his boots. His court martial was scheduled for a week's time, he proudly informed anyone who was interested.

'I hit an officer, bloody had it coming to him,' was the only defence he could muster. The only other occupant of the hut was McIver, a Highlander who spent all day in his bunk complaining of stomach pains, in the vain hope, was the consensus, of postponing his punishment.

We had been taken together, me and Evans, about a mile from the front line outside an estaminet in a small village on the Scarpe River. A Redcap had asked to see Evans' papers as he was attempting to buy a bottle of wine with army money. I could have left him and got away but we were pals and had been for some time. He was short, stocky, and dark — he'd been a miner before the war.

The day before our capture, the Company were in a ditch, you couldn't call it a trench, awaiting the order to advance when the news of the ceasefire had come up the line.

Evans had laughed. 'Bloody hell, not again.'

After an hour, still huddled in the shallow earthwork, and without any orders forthcoming, we noticed that the distant thump of guns had stopped. An eerie silence fell and then, somewhere nearby, a bird chirped. It was as if the order had been confirmed. Some of the men wept out of relief, others sat in stunned disbelief. Most kept well below the rim of the ditch not wanting to 'cop one' at the last. A distant rattle of machine-gun fire restored fear amongst us but then another period of calm settled over the landscape.

'Stay where you are, lads,' came the order from our Officer-of-the-Day, a twenty-two-year-old innocent, as he stumbled over to us.

'Is it true, sir?' asked a young lad, desperation in his voice. He was ignored and I heard him mumble 'Please, God...' and I asked myself, where is God in all this? I knew where the King was. In his country, safe and sound. But God…

After an hour of staying where we were, a strange sense of irony flooded my mind and without even looking to see if I was being watched, I tossed aside my rifle and clambered to my feet. Evans and I were separated from the main body of the Company, what was left of it, by a tangle of barbed wire and a wooden barrier.

'Oy, where are you going?' Evans whispered.

'I'm off home… coming?' And he followed unthinkingly.

We had met at training camp near Hereford. I was drawn to the lively young Welshman and his irreverent humour. When I received my Corporal's stripe and was told not to fraternise with the lower ranks, I ignored the order out of loyalty to those I liked, and Evans and I would often spend time together, going in to town at weekends, drinking in the pubs, fraternising with the locals.

I hadn't asked for the promotion. In fact I told Captain Grimshaw that I'd rather stay in the ranks, but the Captain was convinced that I was "officer material" and made it clear that life could be difficult if I didn't take the promotion.

'Don't make no difference to me,' Evans had said. 'We can still be mates.'

He wasn't married but knew a widow in Port Talbot that he would write occasional letters to. 'Not a looker but good fun, if you know what I mean,' was how he described her. But it wasn't long before he'd formed a relationship with another woman in the town and consequently, I saw less of him.

After the division was posted to France, our friendship revived. The monotony and general degradation of continual marching and life in temporary billets and makeshift trenches brought us closer together. When Evans had been injured by a shell fragment during a brief, pointless bombardment I visited him in the field hospital and wrote to the widow in Port Talbot explaining what had happened and that his right hand was unable to hold a pen.

After several months, much to my relief, I was reduced to ranks. Captain Grimshaw had been replaced after his breakdown following a particularly devastating counter-attack which resulted in the loss of half the company. His replacement, Captain Campbell, was a more ruthless type of officer who mistook my obdurate, often sarcastic, manner for "general insubordination" and had me demoted. When Evans returned to the front line, he was glad to see the stripe gone.

'I knew the whole bloody thing was a mistake,' he said.

'You're wrong. I could have made it, but I wasn't going to play their game,' was my explanation. Evans didn't understand and was unsettled by my broody manner. In truth, two years at the front, where I'd experienced so much death, misery and boredom had given me a new sense of the impermanence and of the futility of it all. The line I had been fed when I joined up about the army being a 'great leveller' was clearly nonsense. The officers lorded it over the enlisted men, received all the privileges, and apart from one or two oddballs, kept well away from any danger.

Just as dusk was falling one day in June 1916, as we were crouching together on the fire-step waiting to go on a sortie, Evans, nervously awaiting the order, asked, 'How come you never write home?'

'There's no one to write home to,' I said. Evans didn't understand.

'But everyone's got someone...' he said and retreated into

himself.

I was twenty-seven years old, but like most of my fellow soldiers after a spell at the front, looked ten years older. I had shaved off a moustache I had grown during my tenure as an officer in the hope that it would give me back some youth as well as some self-respect.

Some hope, I thought as I stared at my gaunt face in the broken glass shaving mirror in our dugout.

My mother — I'd never known my father — had died of tuberculosis when I was two years old and I had been passed on to an aunt who lived in Lincoln. When she died, I was fourteen and the landlord kicked me out but luckily a neighbour who felt for my predicament gave me a room and got me a job sweeping up in a small factory that made parts for steam engines. When the neighbour's husband, a rather timid freckled man, entered my room one night and tried it on, I punched and kicked my way out of a situation that, at first, I didn't understand. The following morning I packed my bag and left.

'Don't neglect your education, lad,' were the last words the man's wife said to me, a pained, resigned expression on her face.

I took a room near the factory where a few of my work mates roomed. The landlady, Mrs Johnston, a tubby, cheerful woman took care of me and provided a good square meal every evening. She also imparted an appreciation of Shakespeare and the Bible to an impressionable teenager. '"Is there no play, To ease the anguish of a torturing hour?" Before I became a landlady, Edward, I trod the boards with Henry Irving's company,' she proudly informed me.

Evening meals were often accompanied by readings from *Macbeth* or *Romeo and Juliet,* her favourite — she had played the nurse.

By the time I was twenty, I had become a semi-skilled engineer and had gained promotion from the assembly line to my own workbench. A lot of my spare time I spent at the local Mechanic's Institute. They had a small reading room, and I engrossed myself in books, mostly about the history of England. I was particularly struck by Macauley's version of events which led me to think about what it was to be English. One particular line of his stayed in my mind, "The measure of a man's real character is what he would do if he knew he would never be found out." I found it troubling. What did he mean? I had taken to attending meetings at the Institute where, on a Tuesday evening, invited speakers would give a talk on a variety of topics. One guest speaker was a young Scotswoman who lectured a small crowd of us on the question of women's suffrage and the evils of alcohol consumption. She had mentioned Macauley during her speech and afterwards I plucked up the courage to approach her. I complimented her on her talk and then asked if she had heard that quote which had stayed with me. She knew it well.

'It was one of his most famous sayings. It has to do with the notion, I think, that we are, or should be, guided by our conscience. Have you read his History of England?' I could only stand there, cap in hand, and admire her forthright manner. I nodded.

'Macauley was a great admirer of Universal Suffrage as practised in America. As for his views on temperance...' And her words faded as she was swept away by the organising group.

More money in my pocket had given me the confidence to venture out on a Saturday night, sometimes with one of my pals from the factory. And it was on one of these jaunts, one rainy November night, that I first saw Celia, a fair-haired, grey-eyed, eighteen-year-old local girl. She sold me a ticket at the theatre to a touring production of *Hamlet*, and I was so struck by her looks that I dropped the change onto the floor of the ticket office and made a fool of myself much to the amusement of my friend Jack whom I'd persuaded to attend. Jack fell asleep during the first act and then left at the interval, but I stayed on, as much for the spectacle as for the hope of seeing again the girl who worked in the box office. As the curtain came down, I hurried past the applauding audience and dashed down to the foyer, but the box office was closed. It was the last night of the play and the company was, so the sign said, moving on to Nottingham. I surprised myself by feeling suddenly distraught. But when I found out from the doorman at the stage door that the box office staff were not part of the company, I felt a certain relief. On my next day off I got to the theatre early and hung around in the cold, waiting hopefully. At eleven o'clock, the doorman arrived, opened up the theatre, and remembering me, let me wait in the foyer. Celia arrived a few minutes later, and yes, she remembered me too and so I bought a ticket for the next production, *The Count of Monte Cristo* which I attended for all of its five-night run. The following Saturday night, feeling emboldened, I asked for a date and took Celia for a meal at the Station Hotel. I saw her home afterwards and we held hands on the tram, but I felt too awkward to kiss her goodnight on the steps to her home even though it was obvious that we both wanted to.

We had been going out together for only two months when Celia was taken by the typhoid epidemic that struck the town through its contaminated water supply. At about the same time, while I was struggling to understand her absence, I was passed over for promotion to full engineer, the post going to a nephew of the factory owner with little experience and less acumen. Up to this time in my life I had not been aware of the class differences between myself and others but this act, as I saw it, of favouritism and downright stupidity, alerted me to a world beyond one of common sense and fair play. I hadn't helped my cause by attempting to interest my fellow workers in the idea of organising some sort of trade union within the factory.

The following day, still angry, I handed in my notice. The General Manager shook his head and made it clear that finding another position wouldn't be easy. I replied that I was willing to take that chance.

I packed my bag, said goodbye to Mrs Johnson and left on a train bound for London. In my bag was the *Book of Common Prayer* which Mrs Johnston had thrust into my hand during her tearful farewell. On the train, having found a seat in third class between a sleeping sailor and a veiled woman draped in black, I opened Mrs Johnson's gift, and on the first page, read: *'That it may please thee to preserve all who are in danger by reason of their labour or their travel, We beseech thee to hear us, good Lord.'*

Lord, indeed, preserve us, my thoughts echoed, and I tucked the small volume into my jacket pocket and gazed out of the window as England sped by.

After a few weeks in London and with my savings almost gone I enlisted in the 4th Middlesex Light Infantry. The predictions of the General Manager had proved only too true. I had mistakenly thought that my experience as an engineer would stand me in good stead but whether it was my provincial accent or lack of "friends" who could have put in a good word that told against me, I didn't know. I began to suspect some sort of intrigue and then reproached myself for it. A pattern of increasing bitterness followed by admonishment made me feel, at times, angry, at other times, sorry for myself. Restless, I moved digs three or four times, each new room costing less than the previous one. I would exist on a measly breakfast, if provided — some landladies didn't — and a sandwich before resuming my luckless search for employment. All the talk on the streets and in the newspapers was of the coming war with Germany and how the munitions factories up North would reap the benefit. It was in the bar of a public house in Poplar one evening that I fell into conversation with a man who said he was a soldier on leave.

'Great life, if you don't weaken,' he said and laughed.

I accepted his offer of another light ale and was surprised to find myself being engaged by stories of a world where merit was rewarded and where, no matter what a person's background, the uniform was "a great leveller".

'With your experience with machines,' he went on, 'you'd 'ave no trouble getting on.'

And so, the following day after a particularly dispiriting interview with the General Manager of a printing works in Farringdon, '...we only take Public School...', I went along to the local recruitment office and joined up.

Chapter 3

'Come on, Burne!' The voice of Sergeant Major Perry barking out woke me. I struggled out of sleep and sat up on the side of the bunk.

This is it then, I thought. To my surprise, I found, in my hand, the *Book of Common Prayer*. I had been reading it the night before. It was the first time I had opened it since that time on the train.

'And you won't need that,' said Perry, pointing at the small black book. 'You've been reprieved, you lucky bastard! That skiving Scot has been carted off to hospital. Bloody M.O. gave him a sick note, didn't he!' he said, sounding a little disappointed as he marched away.

'You too, Groves. Get dressed, half-pack, outside in five minutes.'

It was raining hard. Sergeant Major Perry sat up front with the driver. Groves and I bounced around in the back of the lorry. At our feet were two shovels, a pickaxe and a plain deal coffin.

'Where do you suppose we're going?' asked Groves. I didn't reply, intent as I was on working out a plan of escape, but it didn't seem to bother Groves.

'Bloody army, always getting you to carry out useless tasks.'

I had been planning an escape ever since Evans and I had been delivered to the prison camp. I had reckoned that it was about twenty miles from the coast, somewhere near Cambrai. There weren't many guards on duty that I could see and the wire perimeter fence seemed to have been hastily erected. But finding the right moment had eluded me. We may have been lightly watched over but they kept us busy with futile tasks, cleaning the latrines, polishing the nail-heads. This was the first time I had been outside the camp since Evans and I had been captured, and with only two guards, Sergeant Perry and the driver, I began to see the possibility of flight. It had been my contention from the moment I had been sentenced that the court's verdict was unjust. Evans had accepted the ruling and went to his death uncomplainingly. But even though, during the six months since the war had ended and I had been behind barbed wire, the outcome looked inevitable, I had not given up thoughts of a getaway and of, somehow, getting back to England. It was the sense of unfairness and inequality that nagged at me. What about all the lead-swingers who had evaded the war by foul and corrupt means who were now at home safe in their beds? And when Sergeant Major Perry reluctantly, unknowingly, gave me another chance, I resolved to take my fate in my own hands and cheat the firing squad.

The truck hit a bump in the road and the lid of the coffin fell off revealing a white canvas winding sheet.

'Bloody hell!' exclaimed Groves. Clearly he found the shroud more disconcerting than the coffin. I lifted the flap at the back of the truck and peered out at the flat, murky landscape. *More mud...* I thought, as we turned off onto a dirt track that wound its way down into a hollow amid the rolling ground of what had probably once been farming land.

'Shut that flap, Burne. It's no concern of yours where we're going.' Perry's muffled voice from the cab came angrily.

Presently the lorry slowed, then stopped and the engine died. We had come to rest near a small temporary cemetery. White wooden crosses, about a hundred of them, I reckoned, littered the slope, some still sticking up, others fallen over through lack of care or due to the inclement weather.

Evans and I had seen many such burial grounds during our time in the prisoner-of-war camp. One of our duties had been the occasional digging up and reburial of bodies that had eerily surfaced as the rain turned the ground to liquid mud and wore away the surface of the earth.

A cackling of crows came from a clump of trees nearby. I gaze with hope at the cover provided but the stretch of ground was too great for an attempt. The rain had turned into a fierce drizzle.

Sergeant Major Perry led the way down a slippery path towards the graveyard, Groves carrying the shovels, I the pick and winding sheet. He consulted a scrap of paper as he bent over each marker until he straightened up and pointed.

'Right you two, this one, get digging and careful like.'

'What do you mean, "careful like", Sarge?' Groves asked naively.

'I mean, we don't want him in bits, do we?'

'Who is he?' persisted Groves.

'Never you mind, Private nosey Groves, you just get digging. You, too, Burne!' And he quickly pulled the wooden cross out of the ground and secreted it underneath his cape before I could read the name or number on it. He scowled and turned away, as if bestowing a covert nature on the task at hand. The mound was barely visible above the surrounding earth and it wasn't long before remnants of a grimy, rotten canvas appeared. The shroud was roughly tied by rope around the feet, waist and neck as if bound in haste. Groves was reluctant to pick up the corpse but after various threats from Sergeant Major Perry, we managed to transfer it onto the newer, cleaner winding sheet and I bound the whole carefully with fresh twine handed me by Perry.

'Bloody Lazarus,' muttered Groves under his breath, and as if tainted, he wiped his hands vigorously on his tunic.

'Right, get the box,' ordered Perry and we marched back to the lorry. The driver, a squaddie called Shippey, whom I had seen around the prison camp, was trying to light the stub of a cigarette as we dragged the plain deal coffin out of the rear.

'You get all the best jobs,' he remarked, his laughter turning to a violent coughing fit as we returned to the burial ground. By now we were all wet through. We lifted the body into its new, drier home.

'Not much left of him, Sarge,' said Groves.

'There wouldn't be much left of you if you'd been under the sod for a couple of years,' replied Perry.

I hammered the lid securely on, stepped back and looked around at the bare hillside and the distant clump of trees.

Not here, I thought. *There'll be another, a better place...*

'Right, get him on board,' ordered Perry, and now acting as pallbearers, we carried the coffin back to the transport.

The casket stowed safely back in the lorry, Groves chirpily asked, 'Where to now, Sarge?'

'Get in and shut up, Groves, or I'll have you on a charge.'

We climbed in and Perry lowered the tarpaulin flap after us.

'And no more peeking, Burne,' he repeated forcibly and soon the 'burial party' was on its way again.

Groves, his feet resting callously on their grim cargo lit a cigarette.

'Another pointless bloody exercise! What do you think, Burne? After all you was nearly a dead 'un yourself?'

I smiled at the lad's cheek.

'Yes, something of an irony wouldn't you say?' I replied.

'Dunno about that, not having had no education, like some...'

Where had I heard that accusation before? Then I recalled a meeting with the Commanding Officer just before our company was ordered back into action.

'You've obviously had some sort of education, Burne, and the men like you. Why not put in for a commission? We're short of officers after the last push and it'll get you out of the firing-line, as it were.'

I had declined, of course. I didn't want any favours, no special treatment. Consequently, back at the front "they" made my life as difficult as "they" could by sending me on carrying parties, reconnaissance sorties, anything with a hint of extra danger, as if life in the trenches wasn't dangerous enough. I was talked about as being a troublemaker, a "bolshie". Not knowing what the word meant, I asked the company padre, knowing that a man of the cloth was probably going to tell the truth or something like it.

'Well, Burne... I believe the term refers to recent events in Russia, the revolution and so forth.'

He was clearly uncomfortable talking about it.

'You mean the overthrow of the monarchy, the ruling class?'

'Violence is not the answer, Burne.'

'No? What are we doing here then?' I replied truculently.

He ignored my outburst.

'Nevertheless, Burne, I'm surprised you didn't take a commission. A man of your calibre...'

The padre's words followed me out of the room, and I returned to the relative safety of the trench where my only friend, Evans, consoled me with a smoke and another lewd tale of the widow in Port Talbot. That night, whilst on sentry duty, I considered tossing the *Book of Common Prayer* over into no man's land but thought better of it and instead grabbed a piece of discarded shell casing and hurled that over the lip of the trench. It made a loud splash as it landed in a mud-filled crater. The enemy, only a hundred yards away, heard it too and it drew a burst of machine-gun fire.

About an hour later, the lorry turned off a country road and came to a halt by a small chapel on the edge of a wooded area. The drizzle had now become a steady rain. The flap was lifted and an unusually nervous Perry ordered me and Groves to take our "passenger" inside the building. As we dragged the coffin out, Groves as usual taking the lead, I noticed a large black car off to the side, under the trees. I could just make out a shield and crest on the door. There was no one else about.

The chapel was austere, unadorned, as if, after four years of war, it had given up any pretensions to sanctity. Across the middle of the chamber, in a line, were four trestle tables. Perry indicated the one farthest to the right. Groves, struggling under the weight of the load, headed for the nearest table to the door. 'Does it matter which one, Sarge?'

'I'll give you does it matter. Put it here!'

He then took a tattered Union Jack flag from his tunic, unfolded it and laid it over the coffin.

'What's going on, Sarge?' asked Groves.

'Never you mind. Out!'

Perry ushered us outside and told us to get back in the lorry, '...and stay there!' He pulled down the flap but through the gap that was left I watched him march over to the black car. The chauffeur, a weaselly-faced man, had climbed out and was standing by the car smoking a cigarette. He nodded to Perry as if he knew him. The rear window was wound down; Perry saluted and had words with whoever was inside.

'You'll be for it if he catches you,' said Groves.

'I'm for it anyhow,' I replied. *But not if I can get away,* I said to myself. I looked out at the trees behind the building, natural cover but the rain would make muddy tracks so I would have to stay off any paths...

My plans were interrupted by the return of Perry who pulled the tarpaulin over the gap and climbed into the cabin next to Shippey.

Fifteen slow minutes passed, then, a convoy of three army trucks pulled up and parked alongside.

Intrigued, I watched as three plain deal coffins were carried, each by two uniformed soldiers, from the vehicles to the chapel, in a ritual the same as Groves and I had performed. A group of two officers and a chaplain, gathered together and were approached by Sergeant Major Perry. After a few minutes, the pallbearers came out and returned to their respective trucks, no doubt having deposited their loads on the three empty trestle tables.

The chauffeur threw away the stub of his cigarette and opened the rear door. Two men climbed out, both British Army Officers. Their seniority was evident by the way they were acknowledged by the others. The group moved towards the chapel. There was a brief conversation before one of the officers, I couldn't make out which one, entered the building.

I sat back, baffled by what I had witnessed. However, enthralled as I was, a more pressing impulse took over. If I was going to make good an escape, now was the time. Groves was lighting a cigarette, oblivious to what was going on. I looked into the cab and saw Shippey napping, his head slumped on the steering wheel.

I weighed up my chances and tried to work out in what direction the coast was. I was almost off the bench when the flap lifted and Perry said, 'All right you two. Follow me.' My insides turned. Another opportunity gone.

We climbed out. The three other trucks were driving away as we followed Perry across the open area and around the side of the chapel. In the trees, half-hidden, was an army ambulance. I hadn't seen that arrive with the other vehicles. We were joined by the weaselly-faced chauffeur. Perry led us up to the ambulance and he opened the rear doors. Inside was a large, heavy-looking wooden casket.

'Right, get it out.'

And it was heavy. It took the three of us and we could have done with some help. Perry held open the vestry door and we manoeuvred the casket inside and through to the apse. The four trestle tables were still there, but empty. The coffin we had carried in earlier was still resting on its bier but the flag had gone.

'Here,' barked Perry. He indicated the table next to the coffin and we just managed, with Perry's help, to deposit the casket. 'All right, back to the lorry,' he said to Groves and me. And we left, followed by the chauffeur and Perry.

Outside, the rain was sheeting down. Groves made a dash for the lorry and clambered on board. Perry and the chauffeur hurried over to the black car. The window was still wound down and a small pink face with ginger hair and moustache appeared. One of the officers, I remembered from earlier. I hesitated, and before he could say a word to Perry, he noticed me and withdrew. Perry turned and bellowed at me to obey orders or face a charge. I took off, and reaching the lorry, climbed in.

'Bloody army. More bloody pointless jobs than you could shake a stick at.' Groves lit a cigarette.

Through the gap in the tarpaulin I could see Perry still engaged with the occupants of the black car. After a while, he came over and ordered Groves to put his cigarette out and follow him. There was one more task to accomplish. 'What about me?' I asked.

'You stay put, bloody troublemaker.'

Groves clambered out. Shippey, roused from his dozing, followed them. Now was my chance. I slipped out from under the tarpaulin flap and slid alongside the lorry. It was only a few yards to the edge of the trees and I made a dash for them. Keeping low, I headed off, away from the strange happenings of the day, away from the army and the mud and death. I was going home, and no one was going to stop me this time.

The rain, heavier by now, made the going difficult but I kept away from any obvious paths so as not to leave any footprints. I had worked out, during the hour-long journey, that I had until nightfall before they would come after me and by then, I hoped, I would have gained a channel port. They would know that that would be my likely destination but I couldn't help that. Probably Dieppe was the closest if my sense of direction was accurate. The woods seemed to go on forever and it was just as dusk was upon me that I came across a railway line and followed it for several miles. A workman's hut furnished me with a set of grubby overalls, and a couple of hours later, I didn't look out of place as I strolled into a seaside town and made for the harbour area. My uniform was rolled up in a sack tucked under my arm. It was nearly midnight and hunger was gnawing away at my belly but that could wait. A passage to England was the priority and I casually eyed the ships at anchor, hoping to learn of the next sailing.

A steamer from Ostend seemed the likeliest candidate, and when a group of sailors went ashore, I slipped noiselessly up the gangplank and stowed away in one of the lifeboats. I had scavenged a half-eaten baguette from behind a cafe and I wolfed it down. My hideaway was uncomfortable and cold and sleep, when it did come, was sporadic. The events of the past few days came to me in a jumble of dream-like images, some horrific, some banal, all incomprehensible; white wooden crosses, an empty coffin, Groves' hapless expression, a black car, a black bird circling endlessly. What sounded like a volley of gunshots brought me out of my troubled dream, but it turned out to be the blast of the ship's hooter.

To the sound of seagulls shrieking overhead, I lifted the canvas cover of my hideaway. Out of the mist loomed chalk-white cliffs then a fort overlooking harbour walls. I was nearly home and wondered whether or not word of my escape could have reached England by now. The ship docked and the crew went ashore but I stayed hidden until darkness fell. When all seemed quiet, I cautiously emerged dressed in my still damp uniform which I had, with great difficulty, put on in the confines of the lifeboat. With some foreboding, with boots echoing excessively loudly, or so it seemed to me, Private Edward Burne walked down the gangplank, and after nearly four years abroad stepped onto the solid terrain that was England.

It wasn't easy evading the Military Police who were checking the papers of anyone in uniform but by keeping to the shadows and back streets, I managed to get to the railway station. I had no idea at which port the ship had docked but was pleasantly surprised by the station sign which read, 'Newhaven'. The journey to

Waterloo took about four hours, the train stopping at what seemed every station, and we arrived in the early hours of the next morning. I had spent most of the journey avoiding the ticket inspector by sitting in the toilet. While there I tried to grasp what had gone on in France and understand my role with the "burial party". In my mind I ran through the order of events but could come up with no rhyme nor reason for what had occurred. *Maybe Groves was right and it was just another banal army exercise that no one, least of all those involved, would comprehend.* But then I suspected that there was something peculiar, almost sinister, about the whole affair. However, a more pressing concern soon took over my thoughts, the ache in my empty stomach was now severe and I rummaged through the pockets of my uniform in the vain hope of finding some money, but with no luck. I waited until the train had decanted its passengers before emerging from my hiding place and as I passed through the buffet car I happened to notice a bread roll on the floor under an abandoned table. In desperation, I stuffed it into my pocket. In the doorway leading to the baggage car, I devoured it, almost choking in the process. I mused, with some wry humour, that even stale French bread tasted better than fresh English.

As the platform emptied I looked out from the window of the carriage. The ticket gate was being patrolled by Military and Civil Policeman checking the papers of all soldiers. It was as if they were searching for someone in particular.

Surely, I thought, *they couldn't be looking for me... not so soon, anyway?* A few minutes later, under cover of another trainload of passengers, I climbed down from the carriage, crossed the tracks and made my way towards the cargo area of the station. Dodging the baggage trolleys, I ducked out through an archway that led to the street.

So... they are on my tail. But why all this attention for a deserter?

About an hour later I was sitting on a bench in Russell Square, partially hidden from view by a mass of shrubbery. I had walked briskly away from Waterloo, crossed the Thames at Westminster, and taking the back alleys and side streets, arrived in Bloomsbury. I knew my way around London quite well after my experiences job hunting. The leaves of the plane trees were beginning to fall, the weak sunlight beginning to fade. The darkness couldn't come quickly enough for me. The small cafe in the corner of the square was closing up. For an hour or so I'd endured the aroma of coffee and the smell of bacon that wafted over on the late afternoon breeze. When the shutters were down and the door locked and the lady who served had gone, I ambled over and surreptitiously rifled the rubbish bin. A rasher of bacon and a piece of burnt toast were my only consolation and when I noticed a nanny with a pram watching me with a pitying expression I decided to move on.

Pity is the last thing I need, I thought as I walked along past the crowds who now began to flood the pavements. I envied them, the office workers, the secretaries, the smart businessmen, the shop-girls, envied their freedom, the money in their pockets and handbags, envied their easy-going swagger as they headed for the pubs, cinemas and restaurants. And of course, their homes, wives, and children. I brought myself up short. *Don't get maudlin, Burne.* But it was difficult not to feel the way I did especially after giving four years for King and Country. *And where has it got me? A fugitive, hungry, strapped and tired. If only there was someone I could go to, someone to trust, a friend like Evans...*

A seat at the back of a small cinema — I had entered through a hastily left-open fire door — gave some shelter and a refuge from my pursuers. As the newsreel flickered across the screen —

Queen Alexandra was unveiling a statue to a nurse, I didn't catch the name, my thoughts turned to what it meant to be English. Perhaps it was the music accompanying the film that stirred uncomfortable feelings inside me. Patriotism had not been my motive for joining up but nevertheless there was something — call it "Englishness" — that bound me to this land. Why had my first thought on escaping been a return to England? As I mulled these things over, I noticed an MP making his way down the aisle. I slipped out of my seat and fled by the same fire door that I had entered by. The evening was descending on London and with it a swirling smog.

I left the busy street near Holborn; my aim was King's Cross from where trains went north, but as I looked up — I was in the habit now of walking with my head down lest anyone should recognise or confront me — I saw the blue sign over the entrance to a police station. A pair of constables were coming down the steps. I ducked into an alleyway alongside a graveyard that led to a church. There was a single lamppost dimly lighting the way. I hurried on. It seemed that darkness would be my only friend.

As I reached the rear of the church I glanced back: one of the policeman was turning into the alleyway. A pair of large wooden doors offered possible sanctuary. I grabbed the brass handle, turned it and pushed. With a shudder the door opened and I found myself inside a stone-walled church hall. In the gloom I could make out rows of trestle tables and chairs and at the far end what seemed to be a kitchen area. At one of the tables, under a dim lamp, sat a woman writing in a notebook.

Without looking up, in a tired voice she said, 'I'm sorry, but we're finished for the day.' I could hear the approaching footsteps of the policeman ringing on the cobbles outside and moved further inside the hall, into the darkness. The woman looked up again, perhaps unnerved by my presence, put down her pencil and stood up. As she came closer I could see a plain but not unattractive face, with kind brown eyes and a small mouth.

'As I said…' Her voice, almost inaudible, faltered. Just then the policeman appeared in the doorway. His silhouette spoke.

'You all right, miss?'

She hesitated before answering. 'I'm just closing up, thank you.' Her voice was soft, quiet.

'Beg pardon, miss?'

Ignoring him, she continued looking at me as if I were someone she might know.

The hall was a sort of refuge for down-and-outs, the tables in rows, the kitchen area, the plates and mugs stacked. I had spent time in just such establishments during my days of want in London before signing up. And I recognised the picture on the wall, 'The Light of the World', which seemed to hang in every soup kitchen.

'Is this man one of your… patrons?' the policeman asked. 'No, I mean yes,' she replied. 'He's been helping out.'

'But the gentleman only just came in, miss.'

'He was running an errand,' she said.

There followed a moment of silence. Did he believe her? Feeling uncomfortable under her fixed gaze, I hung my head.

'If you say so, miss. Sorry to have bothered you. Good night.' And he was gone and the door closed behind him, his heavy footsteps receding along the alleyway.

Relieved as well as puzzled I slumped down onto a chair, put my elbows on the table, my head in my hands. 'Thank you,' I managed to say.

She moved closer and sat down opposite me. She leaned forward, and with a gentle movement, placed her hand on my arm. 'William.'

Chapter 4

She lived in a terraced house on the side of Harrow-on-the-Hill overlooking the railway station on the outskirts of London. The Metropolitan Line train took us there after she had locked up the church hall. As we sat together in the virtually empty carriage — it was the last train — she told me how she knew the telegram reporting my death was in error and that it was only a matter of time before I returned. She had a slight tremor in her voice as she spoke as if her nerves were on edge. Her continual gaze in my direction I found unsettling, not being sure if she really believed I was "her William" or whether she was still trying to make up her mind. I played along, seeing as there might be a safe haven in the offing, even if it was only for a few days or until she, Edith was her name, came to her senses and realised her error.

'I was wounded... a piece of shrapnel... in hospital in France... lost my memory...'

She said she understood it all. There had been a case of a man in Liverpool who had lost his memory and when it came back he had gone home only to find his wife had married again and their second child on the way. 'It was in Titbits,' she explained with complete candour.

As we walked up the hill from the station she began to re-acquaint me with a few details from my forgotten past. She had inherited the house from her Uncle Percy on his death, which was fortunate for us as we had only been married for a month and the rooms we had been renting in Neasden were not up to much. The house was a decent-looking terraced house with a small garden front and back and a gabled roof. She reminded me that I worked for an insurance company in Old Street and travelled up to town on the Metropolitan Line every day. I hurriedly said that there was no question of me going straight back to work as my health was not good. She understood perfectly and was only too happy to have "her William" to herself after three years of separation. I added that in light of my experiences, I might not return to the insurance world and might, in time, consider another, more rewarding occupation. She pretended to understand but I could tell that she was slightly unnerved by the prospect. Of course, I realised that the charade would not last for ever and that sooner rather than later I would have to revert to once again being Edward Burne, wanted by the Military Police for desertion. So far, I had been lucky.

We sat in the parlour at the back of the house and Edith prepared a mug of cocoa which I had with a slice of cake. I was ravenous, she could see that. There was an excitement in her every word and deed and while I ate she went upstairs to run me a bath.

I worked out a narrative and when she returned I explained to her that, one night on a working party in no man's land, I had been the victim of an exploding shell that had killed Private Evans, the man I was with, but that somehow I had been spared and I woke up in a field hospital near Étaples a few days later with no memory of who I was or how I had got there.

'I knew it,' she whispered and she took my arm in hers as if to confirm the fact. From then on all I had to say when she brought up an episode in our relationship was that I was sorry, I had forgotten and she understood and hastily corrected herself for fear of upsetting me.

Early on in our time together it had occurred to me that relatives and friends would be a problem if and when they came calling and so I was relieved when she told me that I had no living relatives, my Uncle George having been the last Perkins and she assured me that her only relation was a cousin who had emigrated to Canada. As for friends, she had few, having kept herself to herself since I had joined the army.

'The closest I came to a friend was a neighbour who I became acquainted with but she moved away. She said she'd write, but…' She went on to assure me that if anyone did call she would send them away using my infirmity as an excuse.

The first night at my new home, my refuge, was in the main bedroom at the front of the house. Clean sheets on the double bed, the wardrobe hung with his clothes, his polished shoes, his shaving things all neatly laid out by the washbasin, even a small bunch of flowers in a vase on the table by the window. She let me sleep on my own, perhaps out of a sense of nervous inhibition, of not wanting to rush things, or maybe she knew that I wasn't really her husband returned from the dead and she wanted to keep the pretence going for as long as possible.

She slept in the spare single bedroom across the landing where she had been sleeping, she told me, ever since the telegram had come informing her that 'William Perkins, Second Lieutenant, Sixth Sussex Regiment, was reported missing, presumed dead.' That first night I was glad of the distance between us. I lay in bed, the first proper bed I had slept in for over three years, and I asked myself if it was fate that drove me to that church hall and into Edith's care or was it just good fortune? Either way, I considered my situation, settled down under the weight of the blankets, and soon fell into a deep sleep.

We soon established a routine which suited me and my

fugitive status. She would shop on the morning for the evening meal and the next day's breakfast. Liver and onions was my favourite meal she told me, but I wasn't fond of cabbage. And she always brought back a newspaper; the *Daily Chronicle* was what I read before the war although she found it a little too highbrow for her tastes, she preferred *Titbits* or *The People*. At first I scoured the pages for any news of a Private Edward Burne and three days after I had met Edith and come home with her there was a small item on one of the inside pages.

'...*it is believed that Private Edward Burne, wanted by the Army for absconding from a prison camp in Northern France while awaiting execution for desertion, has made his way to England and is being vigorously sought by the Military Police and other agencies... The Commanding Officer of the prison camp, Major Dowling, told reporters that Burne was a desperate type who had, due to the negligence of the soldiers guarding him, obtained a pair of wire cutters and used them to make good his escape...*'

No mention of the burial party or the business with the coffin. Still, I thought, it was just like the army to get it wrong. After that there were no more articles and I was able to relax somewhat.

By now I had assumed the general appearance of "her William". A framed photograph on the sideboard in the parlour showed a man roughly my age; our hair colour was similar and judging by the clothes in the wardrobe, we were about the same size. He had a moustache which I adopted, mine having been shaved off in the prison camp.

One fine morning, Edith pointed out the vegetable patch in the small garden at the back of the house which William had begun to cultivate before the war. Her intention was clear and I gradually took to weeding and hoeing and planting carrots and onions. William had also been keen on photography, a box Brownie in the wardrobe confirmed his interest but I expressed none myself and she said that, in time, the old ways would return. I wondered how long I had before my 'old ways' would catch up with me.

After a few weeks, the bad dreams returned. I would wake up in a cold sweat, a figure in uniform looming over me, a black bird swirling overhead, a white shroud and the mud… and unable to get back to sleep I would dress and go for long walks over the hill. Edith, wearing her nightgown, was always waiting up for me when I returned and she would say that she, too, had trouble sleeping but I knew from her red eyes that she had been crying, terrified that I might not return. I would try to comfort her, but over that spring and into summer her behaviour became, at times, more and more erratic. We still didn't sleep together as man and wife but she would bring me tea in bed in the morning as if we had done, and she talked of the children we would have — a boy and a girl — when I had recovered and of the holidays we would take to Margate or even abroad, if I could ever face going back "over there", and I realised that sooner rather than later I would have to tell her who I really was and get her to face up to the fact that "her William" was dead.

One evening in early September as we were sitting in the living room after dinner, Edith glanced up from the copy of *The People* she was reading.

'William, you don't wear your uniform these days.' It wasn't a question, more a bald statement of fact, but I sensed a note of regret in her voice. I had not worn khaki since that night she brought me home, and luckily, William's civilian clothes fitted me well enough. I knew where her thoughts were leading though.

William's spare uniform hung in the bedroom wardrobe, all clean, pressed, and shiny.

'There's going to be some sort of special commemoration… for the soldiers, in London, did you know?'

I looked up. I'd read about the forthcoming event, a memorial service at Westminster Abbey.

'Yes, there was an article the other day in the *Chronicle*,' I said.

The paper was a strong supporter of the upcoming ceremony and urged all who had fought to attend.

'Bloody war won't let go, and anyway, I've had enough of burial parties,' I reflected in dumb silence, hoping that she would drop the subject.

'We should go along. It might be good for you. Your bad dreams I mean. The King is going to be there,' said Edith. She expected some sort of response but when there was none the matter was left hanging in the air. Putting on a uniform again was not something I was keen to do but she mentioned the event again a few days later and I realised that she was as eager to go for her own sake as much as mine and I knew that we would attend and that I would, once again, have to put on the uniform of a soldier in His Majesty's Army.

I rarely went out, apart from my midnight rambles, even though I considered my situation to be fairly safe. One day, a couple of weeks after I had been 'rescued', as I was pottering in the back garden, a neighbour poked her head over the fence and said hello and welcomed me back and said how Mrs Perkins had missed me so and how it must be good to be home. I was greatly relieved, but how long had it been since she had last seen me? Edith told me later that Mrs Pooley had lost her husband on the Somme but that they hardly ever spoke, except to say, 'hello and nice day, isn't it?'

As autumn arrived, I became more aware of Edith's increasingly strange moods. She would gaze at, arrange, then rearrange the photographs on the sideboard. As well as William's framed photograph there were others, mostly distant family members she said.

'Don't you remember any of them… from the wedding?' she asked, a hint of desperation in her voice. I shook my head. I felt it was better that I remain honest to her and use the pretence of memory loss rather than begin to engage in discussion about complete strangers.

One gloomy, damp November day, Second Lieutenant William Perkins stepped out with Edith, his 'wife', and they made their way by train up to London. I had been reluctant to go but when I sensed how much it meant to Edith, I went upstairs and put on William's uniform. After all she had done for me, I told myself, it was the least I could do. And I reasoned, sooner or later I would have to take risks.

As we boarded the train, an enlisted man saluted me and awkwardly I returned the salute but after that no one paid any attention to us, although there were quite a number of soldiers in the carriage. The thought crept into my mind that after resisting the Army's attempt to turn Private Edward Burne into an officer while at war I had, in an accident of terrible irony, become a Second Lieutenant in peacetime. My discomfort was compounded by a one-legged man on crutches who got on board at Wembley and sat opposite us. As he arranged his crutches, he looked up at me and gave a rueful smile. I felt an overwhelming sense of guilt, turned my head away and gazed out at the passing rows of houses with their tiny back gardens all neat and tidy as if nothing had changed, as if the war had never happened, as if no one had died.

By the time we joined the crowds in Whitehall, I had become rather unnerved. I was accustomed to a solitary existence at the house on the hill. For days on end, there was just quiet, attentive Edith for company. There were moments when I felt her presence closing in on me and I had to hold my feelings in check. Now, on the streets of London, I felt a different kind of tension. The numbers of Civil and Military Policemen in attendance made me fearful, as if at any moment, one of them might step forward and apprehend me.

We took up a position on the pavement outside of a public house, behind the sombre, unmoving mass standing ten, twenty deep. Edith held onto my arm in a state of nervous anticipation. After about an hour of standing around, from somewhere came the sound of a military band playing a dirge and as the sound came closer, accompanied by the scrape of slowly marching feet, I saw, through the crowd, representatives of the Army, Navy and Flying Corps, of all ranks. They were followed by a gun carriage pulled by six horses. On the carriage was a coffin draped with the Union Flag. The memory of a similar casket, similarly draped, came to me suddenly. A feeling of nausea rose up, I reeled and clutched Edith for support. As the procession came level with us I noticed that Edith, along with the other women, had lowered their heads slightly and the men had removed their hats and caps. Not wanting to bring attention to myself I took 'his' cap off too. Nearby a young boy had climbed a lamppost and was clinging on to get a better view. His mother was supporting him, her arms wrapped around his legs, as she attempted to explain what was going on.

'Because no one knows who he is, he sort of stands for all the dead soldiers.'

'You mean, it could be Jack in the coffin?' exclaimed the boy.

His mother nodded. 'Or your father or Uncle Tom.'

Or it could be Second Lieutenant William Perkins, the shocking realisation came to me and I suddenly felt ashamed.

'There's the King!' Edith's whisper joined the hushed tones of the crowd. Surrounding the gun-carriage were a number of heavily decorated officers, and among them, the King, in uniform, shoulders hunched, giving the ceremony the seal of Royal approval.

I was becoming sicker in my stomach. I wanted to shout out to the crowds, 'It was this deference that got us butchered, this kow-towing to our supposed "betters" that got us...' and I turned away from the spectacle. Edith had bought a small posy of flowers, turned to me and said, 'I was going to... they said there would be an opportunity to lay flowers.'

Flowers for the dead, I thought. *Well, I'm already dead, so...* All I could manage was a weak smile.

In the distance the sound of artillery gunshots thundered. It was a sound I was familiar with, but I thought, *you never get used to that dead sound.* Already I had seen enough. The crowd was beginning to press forward, or was I imagining it? I reached for Edith's support but she was being carried away from me. She turned to look at me and realised from the expression on my face that I was under some sort of strain. I tried to push through the tightly packed mass of bodies but my feet were like lead, much as they had been whenever the command to advance or 'go over the top' came. After a moment, Edith had disappeared, swallowed up by the crowd. I staggered back and fell against the doors of the pub which gave way as if by way of a welcome.

Inside it was almost empty, just the barman cleaning glasses in anticipation of the impending flood of customers, and a drunken soldier in the corner quietly singing to himself. I slumped onto a bench seat near the door.

"'Ere, you all right?' asked the barman and he hurried over with a nip of brandy. I was glad of the drink.

'Thanks,' I gasped. The barman gave me a pitying glance before returning to his task.

Who is he feeling sorry for, me or Second Lieutenant Perkins? Will it always be like this? I thought angrily. I sat still for a few minutes, until I had calmed down, then I crossed to the bar, flung a shilling down, didn't wait for any change and walked out by the side-door entrance.

I was in a narrow side street. The Abbey towered over my left shoulder and I hurried on away from the ceremony, the crowds and Edith. I leaned against a wall and retched as the brandy hit my empty stomach. A few people were about but they took no notice of just another drunken soldier. After a few deep breaths I straightened up and got control of myself. I was still terrified that a policeman or a fellow officer would come to my aid. My only thought was that I must get back to the safety of "home". I calculated that Edith would understand and guess that that is where I would be. I began to walk along the street, the sound of military bands and marching feet receding as I did so.

In my distressed state I hardly took any notice of the large black car parked on the opposite kerb, but as I drew level something caught my eye. On the passenger door a coat of arms that seemed vaguely familiar. On a red shield a black bird. Underneath was an inscription… I staggered as I recalled the chapel in France. I left the pavement and crossed over towards the car. Coming closer, I read the legend in full: *Super omni generis.*

'Something the matter?' The chauffeur was gazing suspiciously at me and I recognised the same weaselly-faced man I had seen standing by the same car in the rain.

I managed to utter, 'What does it mean?' as I indicated the Latin epigraph.

'Dunno,' replied the chauffeur and he opened the door, climbed in and slammed it shut, bringing an end to our brief exchange. I could only stumble away, an excess of thoughts and images crowding my confused mind. I could remember little of the journey back to Harrow but in the margin of a newspaper I found abandoned on a seat, I managed to draw a likeness of the coat of arms that had been emblazoned on the car and an attempt at the Latin inscription.

Edith found me that evening collapsed in a chair fast asleep, my hand clutching the newspaper. She told me she had panicked when she had returned to the pub and found that I wasn't there. The barman remembered the tired-looking soldier but hadn't noticed which direction he had taken after he staggered out.

Oh, my goodness, he was ill and I left him, she berated herself. The train to Harrow seemed to take an age and she was on edge for the entire time. She rushed up the hill, opened the front door and it was with great relief that her worst fears were laid to rest.

That night, after putting me to bed, she moved her things out of the spare room.

When I came to next morning I was surprised to see that the space next to me had been slept in. I recalled nothing. "William's" uniform was folded over the chair, "his" boots on the floor, "his" cap on the shelf. My surprise turned to dismay as I heard Edith coming up the stairs. She entered wearing a dressing gown over her nightdress, carrying two cups of tea. 'William...'

she began, handing over my tea and climbing into bed on her side. '…about yesterday,' she continued, '…about leaving you. I shouldn't have and I want to assure you that it will never happen again.'

I could only mumble, 'That's all right' by way of a reply and she produced the newspaper page with the drawing and handed it to me.

'You were holding this last night. Is it something important?'

'It's nothing, I don't know,' was all I could manage to say. I realised that a new stage in our relationship had been reached. She had nearly lost me and this was her way of binding me to her care and protection. After supper, as the last light was leaving the sky, Edith fetched my old uniform, the one I had been wearing for my escape from France, dumped it into the brazier in the corner of the garden and set alight to it. From the kitchen doorway, I watched my old self disappear in flames. How much, I wondered, did she know? Had she known all along that I wasn't "her William" but had chosen to ignore the fact, preferring a proxy husband to no husband at all? Up until that moment I had almost forgotten that I was Private Edward Burne, a deserter, a fugitive, so all-encompassing had been Edith's hospitality. I didn't tell her about my encounter with the car and the chauffeur, but I knew that, sooner rather than later, I would have to revisit the events of that day in France and find out what part I had played in that strange ritual.

That night we shared the double bed together as man and wife.

Chapter 5

I awoke, shivering. A cold blast of wind was coming in through the window I had broken the night before. I got up and stuffed one of the hessian sacks into the hole and then walked briskly around my cellar prison to try and get some circulation going. Gradually, as I warmed up, memories of that night with Edith entered my mind...

It had not been an altogether satisfactory experience. I felt awkward, even inhibited, and Edith was clearly tense and unyielding. I had had very little experience with women. Celia had been my only steady girlfriend but that relationship had never developed beyond kissing and embracing each other after a night out. There were the local village brothels in France where Evans and some of the other members of the company would visit, but I couldn't summon up the courage to join them. I got the feeling that Edith's awareness of sexual matters was as limited as mine and her inexplicable changes of mood from apparent contentment to quiet brooding, followed by random, pointless chores, were troubling. I recalled that, one evening not long after our visit to London when I had asked her who one of the photographs on the mantelpiece was and she became agitated and said it was her father. Her face darkened and she shifted uneasily in her chair.

'I told you all about it, William, before we were married.'

'My memory is still not...'

'Of course. Forgive me. I was forgetting. You see, after we married, I rarely thought about my life before we met.' After a few moments she composed herself and continued. 'There was a dark, empty house overlooking the Bristol channel. My father was mostly absent, my mother frail, capricious. I was an only child and as I grew up it occurred to me that I was unwanted. When Father committed Mother to an institution for the insane, I was fifteen. He gave me five pounds, a railway ticket to Brighton and the address of his brother, my Uncle George. I never saw him again.'

She paused as the unpleasant recollection passed and then her face brightened... 'It was in Brighton, on the pier, do you remember, William?'

She had bumped into me as I sat in a deckchair and spilt strawberry ice cream over my clean white trousers. I was there on a day trip with a couple of work colleagues.

'Your friends found it funnier than you did, I remember.' She smiled and I returned her happy look as if to say that, yes, I recalled the incident. 'It was a few days later that a telegram came, postmarked Hong Kong. Uncle George read it out. *Mr Edwin Woodhouse passed over, last week. Funeral tomorrow. Please advise.* It was unsigned and 'tomorrow' was now today. I felt no emotion. Uncle George's only remark was a surly one about "foreigners" and a vague allusion to a possible inheritance. But none came. You and I were soon married, and after a few months in rented rooms in Neasden, and much to the indignation of other family members, Uncle Percy, a relative I couldn't recall ever meeting, in his will, left his house to his favourite niece. Those were happy days, William, weren't they?'

She was gone when I awoke the next morning and I didn't hear her downstairs, preparing breakfast as she usually did. I washed, shaved and dressed and it was while I was searching for a fresh pair of socks that I came across a shoe box, pushed to the back of the wardrobe. In it was a service revolver, some bullets and a telegram announcing 'his' death. *'...The Sixth Sussex Regiment, Commanding Officer Major Pitt-Wilson... regrets to inform you...'* A cold shiver ran down my spine. Just as I was returning the items to the shoe box, I heard the front door open and close and I could hear Edith humming a tune as she entered the kitchen and put the kettle on.

A shopping bag with today's lunch, a newspaper and a bunch of flowers was on the table as I walked in. She seemed to be in a good mood, smiling and chatty, and after kissing me on the cheek she told me to sit down and she would make the tea and cook some bacon that she had bought from the butchers. After breakfast, over a second cup of tea, as the cold autumn sun poured in through the kitchen window, Edith, for the first time told me of the events that led up to her working at the church hostel which, in turn, led to our timely meeting, an event she described as miraculous but inevitable.

'You see, I knew you weren't dead, just missing.'

Chapter 6

A sensation, more of foreboding than pity, gripped me as I wondered where, and more importantly how, Edith was. The first streaks of dawn appeared in the sky above the treeline beyond the parkland. Despite my having blocked the hole in the window, it was bitterly cold and I stomped up and down the basement room flapping my arms. The memory of hot, strong mugs of tea with a tot of rum, served up in the dugouts most mornings came to me and I gulped with envy and distaste and then my thoughts returned to that morning in the terraced house and Edith leaning over the kitchen table, cup in hand, an unfamiliar look of contentment on her face and the relating, in the form of a confessional, of her life after my going off to war and before my timely return…

'I moved out of the front bedroom the day after the telegram informing me of your…' she hesitated as the memory came back. 'I couldn't sleep with the now "official" emptiness next to me and made up the double bed, pulled the curtains across the bay window and moved my things into the spare room across the landing. I told myself that as soon as you came back, our life together would return to the way it had been. Not that it had been perfect. Do you remember, William, the pressures over money and…?' Again she hesitated.

Apparently my job at the insurance company was steady and had prospects but I didn't earn much and day-to-day living wasn't cheap. We were lucky that the house had been left to Edith on the sudden death of her uncle Percy. And that led to another argument over the transferring of the title deeds to my name. But why she had implored? Evidently William was a stickler for the right and proper way of doing things.

'It's only fitting that I, as head of the household, should...'

Eventually William won the argument and at considerable expense, a solicitor was engaged and the matter was settled.

'You weren't mean, William, just careful and do you remember how you would scold me for spending too much on lamb chops or liver and flowers for the living room...? I loved to come down in the morning to the smell of fresh cut flowers, I still do... but we would always make up and sit in the back room after supper, arms wrapped around each other and watch the light leave the sky over the church on top of the hill.'

I nodded in agreement. What else could I do? Unwittingly, or knowingly, she had given me a place of refuge when I most needed it and for that I was grateful and beholden. And I could see that in the telling she was unburdening herself of feelings that she had been unwilling to face up to before the war.

'Often, when we had enough saved,' she continued, 'I would place any loose change from shopping into a jam jar and we would go to the cinema that had opened in the town. We would hold hands and watch the images flicker across the screen and I would wonder how it was that such a spectacle could unfold. Afterwards as we strolled home you would try and explain the process by which celluloid captured light — you were interested in photography and were saving up to buy a camera — but I wasn't concerned with technical matters, preferring to let my thoughts linger on the story that had kept me enthralled for what seemed an eternity but had, in fact, lasted little more than an hour and you had chided me for my silly notions. The story was rather implausible, you would say. I didn't contradict you, just took your arm and wondered if life could ever be as tragic as that of the heroine on the screen.'

Her face darkened again, but in a different way, now more regretful than bitter.

'After four years together, and no children... and after blaming each other and an unhelpful visit to the doctor, we came to an uneasy truce, and if the truth were known or admitted, after you volunteered and left for training somewhere near Wales, I was secretly glad there were none fearing that, on my own, I wouldn't be able to cope. When William Perkins, now a Second Lieutenant in the infantry, was posted to France I knew I'd be fine despite Mrs Cooper next door with three toddlers of her own telling me that the kids were a comfort, her husband having walked out on her just before the last one had been born. Don't laugh at me, William, but I carried on cooking for us both for about a week after the telegram came, it just seemed the right thing to do. Supposing that I had suddenly heard your key in the front door and you had come home on leave and expected a meal. But eventually your portion was thrown away and I soon managed to cut down to just enough for one. Then, I told myself, that when you did return I could say that I had taken my meal earlier in the day and had been expecting you and things would go on as before. I still laid a place for you on the kitchen table facing the window where you liked to look out at the vegetable patch you had begun digging and planting before you went away.'

I remember gazing out at the vegetable plot, now overgrown and weed infested. I was aware of how she kept referring to 'our life that had gone before', and how those few years together were a kind of ideal for the future, and I remembered feeling guilty knowing that sooner or later I would have to be honest with her. Edith poured me another cup of tea and went on with her tale. She was clearly intent on letting me know every detail of her life while I had been at war.

'After a few weeks in the spare bedroom I was sleeping well enough and took to visiting the front bedroom, usually on a Sunday evening, just to check that everything was ready for your return. Your dark blue suit hung next to your spare uniform; your peaked cap was on the top shelf; your boots on the floor of the wardrobe, just as you had left them. I would gently run my fingers along the sleeve and under the collar of the spare khaki uniform and rub the brass buttons between my thumb and forefinger and I would feel somehow comforted. On the shelf behind your cap was a cardboard shoebox. On my first visit to the empty room I had wanted to remove the lid and peer inside but thought better of it... perhaps William would not approve... I told myself and resisted the temptation but on subsequent visits the impulse pestered away in the back of my mind. One hot July day, a few months after the telegram came, a letter from his commanding officer arrived explaining that because of the length of time he had been posted as missing and since no body had been found he was pronounced officially dead... "killed in action".

'One day, I think it was a Tuesday, I gazed out of the open back door, into the garden. It was almost white with the blazing heat. The sound of insects humming and buzzing and the distant wail of a train crept across the threshold. As my eyes became accustomed to the light I noticed the vegetable patch overgrown and parched and came to the conclusion that a mistake had been made. They often were. I'd read only the day before in *Titbits* about a soldier who'd unexpectedly returned home to find his wife had remarried. My William may have been captured, I told myself, and interned in a camp somewhere. Or he could be injured and in a field hospital and sooner or later his whereabouts would be known. "Of course, he's alive. I've got his room ready for his return," I said to myself.

'The following day I began once again to prepare an evening meal for us both. And as six o'clock approached I went to the mirror in the hall and checked that my appearance was acceptable. "An interesting face..." was how you described me on one of our early dates together. A year later the war came to an end and William had not returned nor had there been any further news. But by then I had been working at the mission for about a month. The position — it could hardly be called a job — had come about in a most casual way. Standing in the queue at the butchers one morning I noticed that the lady in front of me had bought the last of the liver.

'William's favourite, and I sighed inaudibly to myself. A loud voice came from behind me. "What time do you have to get here to get a decent cut of meat, then?"

"Sorry ladies," replied the butcher. "It'll have to be a piece of scrag-end or I've got some nice fresh tripe." I turned my head and my gaze fell upon a tall, spindly, angry looking woman dressed in a black coat and hat who turned a disapproving eye on me, and in a panic, I ordered a quarter of tripe.

"Perhaps I should get here before the shop opens, Mr Blowers, to make sure of a proper portion?" the angry lady continued.

"Always glad of your custom, Mrs Crale," he shot back cheerfully.

I was on the pavement outside the butchers, the tripe in my basket, checking over my shopping list, when the same strong voice made me start and I looked up.

"Silly old bugger. He takes the best meat and sells it on the black market. Everyone knows, but what can you do?"

"Oh, I wanted tripe anyway. I find it very nourishing," I said politely.

"Don't you live in Twyford Crescent, the house with the climber on the back fence?"

"Yes, it's a honeysuckle."

"We back on to you. I say 'we'. My husband was killed and I haven't got used to him not being here."

"Oh, I'm sorry."

"Don't be. He was a useless bugger. In truth I'm better off without him. Except for the money side of things, that is." 'Having a missing partner in common, I became friends with Vera Crale and we would shop and then take coffee together on Tuesday and Thursday mornings at a café in St. Ursula's Road opposite the school playground. Vera had a part-time job at a church mission in Holborn, which kept her occupied on Monday, Wednesday and sometimes Friday.

"It's only serving soup and cups of tea to people down on their luck but it keeps me busy and some of the old gentlemen have a tale to tell."

When Vera added that some of them were in uniform, I was immediately intrigued. I found her amusing in a rather vulgar way; she had a story about everyone in the neighbourhood and wasn't afraid to malign them. When I was on my own, I would wonder what stories Vera told to the neighbours about me.

'One morning over coffee and a stale pastry at the café, Vera announced that she was giving up the house and was going to live with her sister in Folkestone. "I just can't afford to stay on here any longer."

"Oh,' I replied, in a rather dismayed tone. "When are you going?"

"This Saturday… and I've yet to find someone to take my place… I'm sorry." She hesitated, then took a breath and said, "To tell the truth, Edith, I've really enjoyed our little get-togethers and when I'm settled I'll send the address and you can come and visit. You'll like my sister, she's like me. Two peas in a pod, as they say."

'That evening, after a meal of tripe and onions, which I'd only half-eaten, I sat thinking about what Vera had said and musing about the job at the mission that was falling vacant. I don't know what made me, but on an impulse I put on my coat and hat, and despite the rain, walked briskly round to Vera's house, knocked on the door, obtained the necessary details and with Vera's "I'll put in a word for you, Edith. Good luck!" ringing in my ears, returned home, a little scared but triumphant.

'The following Monday, at nine o'clock in the morning, I reported to Reverend Williams, the elderly vicar at St Lawrences', an anonymous-looking building near the Holborn viaduct. The hostel was an old hall off a narrow alleyway to the rear of the church. A few stone steps led down from a large wooden door to the main, low-ceilinged area which was laid out with trestle tables and chairs spread out over an uneven stone floor. The kitchen was a small space at the far end of the hall.

'Mrs Howard, the canteen supervisor, a stout middle-aged widow with a glass eye, took me through the routine. "Don't talk to the men — they're mostly men, it can upset them, seeing as they don't like to take charity," she explained. A picture of the King hung on one wall, near the stairs, next to a door which led to a washroom. A faded print of Jesus holding a lantern hung by the window onto the street over which hung dirty grey net curtains. There was barely enough room in the kitchen to prepare anything what with the tea urn and large soup colander and bowls, plates and mugs taking up most of the surface area, but I soon got the hang of things with the help of Noreen, a fourteen-year-old orphan, who seemed to live in the kitchen, she was always there when I arrived in the mornings and was still there when I left in the afternoons.

"Don't you have a home to go to, Noreen?" I asked her one day.

"Yes, but it ain't nothing to boast about," Noreen blurted out in her hoarse, high-pitched voice and I decided to enquire no further. But she was a hard worker and kept her head down and seemed to take to me in her own diffident way.

'The two of us would prepare the soup, usually vegetable, in the morning, Mrs Howard having done the shopping at Borough Market first thing. The doors were opened, and tea was served from ten o'clock onwards. There were always people waiting in the alleyway when I arrived at work and by ten, the number had doubled to about a dozen. Mrs Howard did no more than supervise, swinging the bunch of keys that hung from her belt in a manner calculated to terrify the poor wretches that shuffled down the steps and took up their places.

'As Noreen refused to leave the kitchen while "those disgusting old men" were out there, the service fell to me, who, for three hours after midday, was rushed off my feet delivering bowls of soup and chunks of bread to the assembly which on some days swelled to as many as twenty. Mrs Howard had been right; they were mostly men. Now and again a bedraggled old woman would join them but would never stay long, as if she felt inhibited by the company. At about two o'clock, before the crowd could disperse, Reverend Williams would appear and lead the men in a hymn followed by a prayer. I noticed that this communal act seemed to have little effect on the assembly and as soon as the Reverend had finished they would fall silent and leave, slowly climbing the steps to the outside world. Sometimes a soldier in uniform would uneasily cross the threshold and sit down, always apart from the others. I would take more care serving him, lingering for a moment after placing plate and spoon down in the hope that he might look up, or mumble thanks, but the humiliation must have been more keenly felt by a man in uniform and the few that did come seemed never to return.

'After a week and ignoring Mrs Howard's advice, I began to speak to the men, especially if they were in uniform. At first I would whisper a 'here you are,' or 'how are you today', as I dispensed the food and drink, but I became bolder and when I recognised the regular customers I would greet them and ask how they were. At first the men were taken aback but I persevered and soon the room livened up with mumbled talk and sometimes gruff humour.

'A month or so into my time at the mission, I took to going in on Tuesdays and Thursdays as well. Mrs Howard didn't seem to mind at first and once she realised that I was more than competent began to have the odd day off. Despite returning home exhausted every evening I would bake some biscuits or a sponge cake to take in with me the next day for the men to have with their tea.

"You're spoiling them," Mrs Howard warned. "It won't be appreciated." But I just smiled and carried on with my work.

'Gradually, as word got around on the streets outside, more people down on their luck began to attend the mission. Mrs Howard complained to Reverend Wilson about the strain the increased numbers were putting on her and her staff and recommended that I be, somehow, "spoken to". The Reverend removed his spectacles and listened to his supervisor patiently while staring down at his feet, he had always found her glass eye rather unnerving. He made a visit to the basement later the same day, observed the tables full of clients — he liked to call them 'clients' — and the good cheer that was being dispensed along with the tea and biscuits and promptly relieved Mrs Howard of her duties saying that a much younger woman was needed.

'That woman was me.'

The memory of Edith, and the obvious pride that the job at the mission gave her, came back to me. She tried to hide her feelings under the pretence that she was only doing it for 'his' sake, confident that, one day, 'he' would walk back into her life. But I sensed that her motives were not altogether unselfish and that she found the work fulfilling. She went on...

'Noreen promptly left as well, having been engaged by Mrs Howard, and a new helper, Grace, was taken on to help with the serving and washing-up. Grace was from Lancashire and had come to London to find the soldier that had made her pregnant. But she didn't find him, lost the baby and decided to stay in London on account of her father said she'd brought disgrace on the family and wouldn't be welcomed back. I liked her good humour and frankness, and more importantly, she was a good worker.

"You married?" asked Grace one day during a lull.

"Yes."

"He don't mind you working, then?"

"Actually, he's in the army."

"Oh. In France, is he?"

"Yes, but he's missing. I mean, he's alive but in hospital or captured or something." Grace didn't seem to understand and

68

dropped the subject but she must have said something to Reverend Williams because a few days later he took me aside and commiserated with me and asked if I would like to say a prayer for my husband's safe return. He had a habit, I noticed, of taking off his spectacles and cleaning them on a handkerchief whenever he talked to anyone close-up as if he couldn't bear to see them too clearly at such range.

"No thank you, Reverend."

He looked up, surprised.

"It's not that I don't believe that praying works, just that I don't think it would work for me," and I returned to my duties.

'Reverend Williams was clearly puzzled by my reply, perhaps it smacked of the agnostic, but he said nothing, and placing his clean spectacles back on the bridge of his nose, walked away gently shaking his head. Maybe, I thought, he will console himself with the knowledge that I may have abandoned God but through my hard work the mission had increased the numbers at communion by some measure.

'I threw myself into the work and before long was arriving earlier than Grace and leaving after she had gone. After unlocking the front doors every morning, an hour earlier than my predecessor, I hung the keys on a nail in the kitchen. I didn't want to intimidate the men as Mrs Howard had done by rattling them as I made my rounds.

'One Sunday evening, I was in the front bedroom looking over William's spare boots and uniform and blowing the dust off the brogue shoes he wore for work, when a thought came to me: *He's lost his memory.* In *The People's Friend* only the day before, I had read the story of an officer who had turned up in Liverpool and started life afresh but was hit by a bus and his memory came back and he didn't recognise his new wife. And suddenly the tragedy of it all became clear to me. Lieutenant William Perkins had been in a trench and a shell landed and knocked him over and he had lost his memory of who he was and that he was married to me and of our life together. Then I knew that one day, when the war was over, he would turn up on the doorstop in a forlorn state and I would nurse him back to health. His memory would gradually return, and we would go on as before.

There it was again, that phrase that she continually threw up, 'go on as before'. Sometimes it frightened me, but I had to remind myself how lucky I had been. After my 'rescue' as she termed it, she had, much to the Reverend Williams chagrin, handed in her notice at the hostel, giving as her reason that she would now have her hands full caring for her husband.

By now, after walking around my place of confinement, my body had warmed up and my mind too. What was I to do about my predicament? And about Edith's? I racked my brains to try and figure out how they had found out about her, and why involve an innocent? I didn't care about my own fate, but Edith, well, she wasn't a strong person and her mental state was precarious at best.

The dawn was slowly coming up. I pulled the sacking from the broken window and let in some fresh morning air and recalled the day I had decided to do something about my time in France with the strange burial party.

Chapter 7

A bad night of recurring dreams had brought on a restlessness which resulted in another nocturnal wandering over the hill and around the town. I returned just as first light loomed. Edith was waiting anxiously for my return.

Over breakfast I announced that I had some business to attend to in London and would travel up later.

'Later today?' she asked, trying to hide the anxiety in her voice. I could sense the feeling of dread that swept over Edith.

'Oh. How long will you be gone?'

'I'll be back this evening.'

'Perhaps I could come up with you, William?'

'I think you'd be bored. It's an army matter. I want to look up an old friend I served with.'

She was surprised. 'Oh, does that mean your memory is beginning to come back?'

I hesitated for a moment. 'Just this one pal. A Welshman named Evans.' Although my conscience told me that I should explain my mission, I knew I couldn't say more without betraying myself. 'Something happened in France. I have to know what it was all about.'

Maybe because she didn't want to seem over-protective she let the matter drop but now she was restless and spent the time while I was getting ready pacing up and down in the parlour. *What if he doesn't come back... what if I lose him again... what if...?* She worked herself into such a state of mental agitation that her tears ran effusively and her body stiffened. I heard her weeping, came downstairs and was shocked at her condition. It didn't help that I was wearing 'his' uniform. I had seen this kind of reaction in the trenches, sometimes before an attack, more often afterwards. "Shell shock" was made light of by the military, most considering it a lack of courage, "backbone" as they called it. But as more and more officers began to suffer from the disability, attitudes slowly changed. I had had a run-in with the regimental medical officer who passed a young private as fit for duty when the sixteen-year-old was in a state not much different from the one Edith was in, the tears, the rigid body, the staring eyes.

For four years on the front line I had got used to a uniformity of emotions. Everyone was either frightened of dying or relieved not to be dead. The only exceptions were those who suffered from war weariness, symptoms which I recognised now and again in Edith. I reminded myself that my situation was temporary. Once I felt that the military authorities had given up on me, I would leave and return to my former life. But what was it, my former life? An apprentice engineer with little experience, three years in the army, no home or family.

After a feeble attempt to console her with a perfunctory embrace, I left the house. It didn't help my case by wearing 'his' uniform but it was necessary for the tasks at hand. Why did I feel guilty? Sitting on the train going in to London it occurred to me that perhaps, in Edith's heart of hearts, she knew I was an imposter and that the day I didn't return would be the day she would have to face the truth and that thought terrified her.

Before enlisting, when I was a job-seeker in London, a lot of my time had been spent keeping warm and dry in libraries local to wherever my rooms were located. I had continued my interest in England's history but what had begun, before the war, as a casual pastime became something of an obsession. 'Why,' I had asked myself, 'was England the way it was with so many out of work and the differences in social standing so marked?' And what about that sense of Englishness that I had felt? Did a coal miner, a mile beneath the surface of the earth, feel it in the same way as a Peer of the Realm, safe and secure in his lordly mansion? These feelings were no doubt brought on by my jobless circumstances and the lack of money in my pocket.

I headed for the Central Library in St James. I remembered that they had a comprehensive reference collection and before long, I was searching through a catalogue of heraldic coats of arms. I had kept the rough sketch I had made on the newspaper that day and unfolded it and laid it out on the bench next to me. Eventually, after about an hour, I came upon a shield, a black bird on a red background, underneath the legend, *"Super Omni Generis"*. Baronetcy of Courtney-Allyn, est. 1348. Hopeswell Hall, Huntingdonshire. On the back of the newspaper I made a more accurate drawing and jotted down the details. Energised by my discovery, I left St James Square and swung down Pall Mall and across to the War Office on Horse Guards Avenue.

An elderly uniformed corporal gave me a quizzical look when I asked for the records of the 4th Middlesex Light Infantry.

'You're not one of them,' he said, studying my uniform. I'd overlooked the fact that Second Lieutenant William Perkins was from the 6th Sussex Regiment.

'Pal of mine I teamed up with after Arras...' I blurted out. 'Got separated, thought I'd look him up. Name of Perry...' He directed me to the second floor where, with the help of a less alert young new recruit, I found two soldiers with the surname Perry. One had been a Private, the other a Sergeant Major.

'Oh, we're not allowed to give out personal information,' the youngster said after my request.

'Pity,' I replied, 'saved my bacon at Arras, pushed me into a crater, never got a chance to thank him.'

He hesitated, still mindful of orders. Well, I remembered, you are when you're a newcomer.

'Did you serve... over there?' I ventured, knowing full well that he probably hadn't even made basic training camp. I succeeded in making him feel contrite and the offer of a cigarette, 'take two', which he tucked into his top pocket, 'for later', he explained, persuaded him.

'Just this time and because you took part...' He wanted to know more of my experiences and I was happy to provide a few facts about life in the trenches. 'It was mostly really boring, wet and cold, waiting for the next bombardment or sortie...' I could see his interest fade and as soon as I had Sergeant Major Perry's details, I left.

On the bus to Hackney I complimented myself on the ease with which I had accomplished things so far. How I was going to proceed when faced with Sergeant Major Perry was another matter and I wondered whether or not my 'disguise' would deceive him. As it turned out I didn't have to face him. The address I had been furnished with took me to a street of grimy, squat, terraced houses. I knocked on the door of number twenty-seven and it was a few minutes before a neighbour informed me that I'd missed them. My bewildered expression led to an explanation.

'Twenty minutes ago. If you 'urry you might catch the last knockings.'

My look didn't alter.

'The burial!'

I was surprised and shocked. Death, it seemed, had once again intruded on my affairs.

'Served with him did you?'

I nodded.

'Decent sort, liked a drink or two, 'ardly had time to enjoy his retirement.'

'What was it that—?'

She interrupted, only too glad to go into the grim details. 'Kidneys packed up, that and the accident...'

Just then the door of number twenty-seven opened and a small child, wearing a grubby print dress, stood there. 'They've gone. My mum says I shouldn't open the door.'

'Accident?' I enquired.

'And it wasn't an accident,' the child went on.

The neighbour laughed and disappeared behind her front door. I looked down at the little girl, she must have been eight or nine. 'What do you mean?'

'My mum says to tell anyone who asks that it wasn't an accident.'

'Your father?'

'My grandad. He was in the army.'

'What's your name?'

'Joyce.' She looked me up and down. 'You're a soldier, too.' It wasn't a question.

'That's right. I served with your grandfather in France,' which was almost the truth.

My interrogation was cut short by the return of the mourners, Joyce's mother amongst them. All I could get out of her as she bundled the child inside was, 'and if they think twenty quid will shut me up...' As they filed into the house, about a dozen of them dressed in black, a familiar face caught my eye. A freckled face beneath a shock of ginger hair. Groves, my fellow gravedigger. My initial impulse was to grab hold of him and ask a few pointed questions… but given the circumstances, that was impossible. I backed away and watched the last of the mourners disappear and the door close.

I repaired to the pub at the end of the street, bought a pint of brown ale, sat in the corner and wondered what my next move should be. And what did Joyce's mother mean by '…twenty quid to shut me up?' I was just finishing my drink when the door opened and two men came in and walked to the bar. One of them was Groves, now grinning in that careless way he had and which I recalled from our time in France. I got up, and my heart in my mouth, crossed to the bar. Would he recognise me? It was a risk I had to take. As I waited to be served, a familiar voice rang out.

'Let me buy you a drink, soldier.'

I turned. 'Thank you. A half of mild.'

There was not a hint of recognition in that unthinking face. I remembered that he was in prison for striking an officer, an offence that would have led him in front of a firing squad. How did he survive that sentence, I asked myself?

'Us vets got to pull together,' he continued. 'Where did you see action?' He wandered over and lent on the bar next to me.

'I was at Wipers.' I commented on his smart outfit.

'Funeral. My old Sergeant Major. Looked after me, he did. Got me a job when I was demobbed.'

'That was decent of him'.

'Decent sort he was. Like a father to me.'

I offered to buy him and his friend, a surly looking middle-aged man, a drink.

After some polite banter, I placed a half-a-crown piece on the bar.

'I expect she'll get his army pension,' I ventured.

'Who?'

'His widow. I mean, now that the breadwinner in the family has gone.'

'He was out of work when...' Groves stopped himself, a guilty look on his face.

'How did he cop it?' I asked.

'Bloody car came out of nowhere...' his friend, who had remained silent until now, blurted out. Groves shot him a sour look, tossed down the last of his beer and hustled his friend out of the pub.

With more questions than answers buzzing around in my head, I returned, late that evening, to the house on the side of the hill and Edith.

Chapter 8

The cellar door opened noisily and I was taken upstairs by Roberts to a small room where, at a rough wooden table, I was given a plate of bread and jam and a cup of tea. I guessed that I was near the kitchen area as the stale smell of something having been cooked hung in the air. There was no sound other than birds chirping from outside the window, no activity to indicate people at work.

After all, I thought, *a place like this must have an army of servants to keep it going.*

My thoughts were still of Edith and her plight and I decided that, my own situation being fairly hopeless, I had little to lose any more by being servile.

'Too early for his lordships, then?' I enquired of Roberts who stood over me, the ever-present shotgun under his arm. He didn't reply but shuffled uneasily and I could tell that my question had nettled him. I finished eating.

'Thanks, that was good. I pushed the plate across the table. 'What happens now... a stroll around the grounds?'

My invitation was ignored. I stood up and went to the window. A bank of cloud was rolling in across the lake. I turned to face my taciturn guard.

'Did you serve?'

He looked at me, and after a few moments, his rigid manner seemed to ease a little.

'I'm not supposed to talk to you.'

Sensing a willingness on his part to converse I pressed on.

'In the army, were you?'

'I was the Baron's batman.'

'Of course. In France?'

'And at Gallipoli.'

'Oh, I hear that was a bit of a disaster.'

'Second wave, never even made it onto the beach.'

I laughed. 'Lucky for you both.'

'Lucky?' He seemed suddenly to remember his duties and jerked the shotgun in my direction. 'Unlike you… a deserter.'

'My luck may have run out, but what about the woman? Is it fair that she should be answerable for my actions?'

'It's not for me to say. The Baron is a magistrate. He will decide.'

'That's it. Hide behind the feudal mentality.'

'I don't know what you mean.'

'Thousands of years of knowing one's place. Of fawning and toadying to one's supposed betters, is what I mean.'

'It's the natural order of things.'

'Who says?'

He was, no doubt, about to utter another defence of his calling but approaching footsteps cut him short and he returned to his mute state. The Baron entered. He glanced disapprovingly at Roberts before turning to me. He was wearing a tweed suit, mustard-coloured waistcoat, white shirt and tie, cavalry-twill trousers and highly polished brown brogue shoes. He looked every inch the country squire and local bigwig.

'Well, I trust you have decided to do the sensible thing.'

This was not a question but a statement of fact. His self-belief was breathtaking. I said nothing in reply. He glanced down at the empty plate and mug on the table. 'I see you've been taken care of.' Again, not a question.

I maintained a defiant silence. It was time for Baron Courtney-Allyn to explain to me why I was here and what he suspected me of.

After a few minutes of awkward looks and body shifting, he spoke.

'Your silence condemns you. And also the woman.'

I tried to conceal my disquiet at the mention of Edith.

He went to the window and looked out. 'Sixteen hundred years of history are buried out there. Sixteen hundred years of Courtney-Allyns have found a resting place on this, their land. Some died far away, in the service of their king and country, many died here, in Hopeswell Hall. I had two sons. Roland, the youngest, whom you've met.' Again, the slight falter in his voice.

'My eldest son, Raymond, died at the Somme…' He hesitated, cleared his throat and continued. 'He was brilliant, a classics scholar, rowed stroke for the eights at Cambridge, destined for high scholastic honours, and no doubt, even higher diplomatic office.' He turned away from the window and fixed me with a hostile look. 'Raymond was the perfect embodiment of the ruling class.'

It was the first real show of emotion that he had betrayed in my presence. He quickly regained his poise. 'Do you know what the family motto means?

I knew it. I had read it in the library in London, but I said nothing. What could I say? They seemed to know everything.

' "*Super Omni Generis*", "Class Above All",' he stated with great pride. 'But of course you knew that didn't you, Private Edward Burne? It was written on the piece of paper that Roberts relieved you of when he caught you snooping. That's what gave you away. Your absurd depiction of our family crest.'

Foolishly, I had brought my scribblings with me to

Huntingdonshire in case I lost my way and needed verification as to the whereabouts of the Courtney-Allyns' country seat. My insides churned. My time was up. I wondered how they were going to dispose of me... and of Edith. What of her? It seemed futile to continue with any more evasiveness on my part. I took a deep breath and cleared my throat.

'I suppose I shall be shot whilst evading Roberts in the woods hereabouts. In the gloomy light of early morning. Tomorrow morning, perhaps? And probably, found with a dead rabbit stuffed into one of my pockets. The gamekeeper bags the poacher. A simple case for 'Your Honour' to preside over?'

There was no reaction, not a flicker of understanding from the Baron. Roberts, over in the corner, shuffled his feet awkwardly.

'But what about the woman... Edith, if you didn't already know her name. She is going to be a little more difficult to deal with, isn't she?'

The Baron gave the hint of a smile then sat down opposite me at the table.

'You are somewhat of an unusual type for your class. I mean, you possibly have had some education.'

What was he playing at now? I quickly made up my mind that I wasn't going to enter into any rapport with him. When the time came I would go on my terms, not his.

'All right. You've a right to know what you are accused of and why. Let us begin with the day before yesterday. You were found by Roberts, here, at the family vault. What did you hope to find there, I wonder? A certain emptiness perhaps? And you would not have been disappointed...'

PART TWO

Chapter 1

'The Right Reverend apologises for his absence. A summer cold.'
The curate smiled deferentially and took a seat behind the large
desk which occupied the centre of the wood-panelled study.

Baron Courtney-Allyn sat opposite him, restlessly twirling
his cap in his hand. He had been kept waiting far too long and
was angry that the Dean himself had not received him.

'But what are the Dean's thoughts on this matter?' he
insisted.

'Well, sir, I couldn't possibly—'
Courtney-Allyn interrupted him.

'Come on, don't pretend that you are anything other than
what you are.'

The Curate reddened and lowered his head. Courtney-Allyn
didn't like dealing with subordinates and stood up impatiently.

'I don't know what you mean, sir?' said the Curate.

'Don't play games with me. Is His Grace for it or against it?
You, as his personal secretary and confidante, must know.'

'Well, on the whole, I believe... for, but with certain, shall
we say, *stipulations*.'

'But he knows there is little time left. I don't understand the
delay.'

He had made the journey down to London that morning and
had deliberately worn a respectable tweed suit with a yellow tie
and brown brogues, clothes, he surmised, that would lend the
meeting a less formal air. Now he wished he had come in his

Brigadier's uniform.

The Curate, seeing an opportunity to give his position more authority than the Dean allowed, and sensing the Baron's frustration, produced a letter from amongst the papers neatly arranged on the desk.

'The Right Reverend has already mentioned the possibilities indicated in the letter to one or two of his fellow peers, which is why I thought you should see...' and he handed it to Courtney-Allyn who took it, walked over to the window, and put on his reading glasses.

After carefully digesting the contents, he turned and asked, 'Do we know this Railton chap?'

'We know of him, sir. He is the vicar of a parish near Margate. He was, apparently, an Army Chaplain during the war. In France, somewhere, which is where he got the idea.'

'Well, the word "comrade" will have to be substituted for something less incendiary.'

Courtney-Allyn turned back to the window and stared down into the Dean's Yard, the late afternoon sun cast long shadows, there was a stillness in the air.

The Curate continued. 'It was his Reverence's opinion that someone, in an official capacity of course, should be informed.'

'Then, you'd better pass it on to someone in an official capacity,' he said brusquely as he strode across the room. He handed the letter back to the Curate and added, 'I would prefer it if our conversation, here today, was kept just between the two of us, and His Reverence, of course. For the time being, that is.'

'I understand completely.' Again, the deferential smile and he replaced the letter with the others. Courtney-Allyn took off his glasses, returned them to the pocket of his jacket and walked swiftly out.

The Curate was relieved to be alone. He went to the window, and just to make sure, watched Courtney-Allyn cross the precinct and disappear into the blackness beyond the Chapter House.

Now came the difficult part of the undertaking, to convince the Dean — who didn't have a summer cold but was extremely uneasy about the whole affair — that he need not worry, that his role would be a titular one only and that his reputation, should anything go wrong, be unsullied. He put on his cape and hat and left the study dreading the coming meeting with his superior.

The Baron emerged on to the side-road that ran alongside the Abbey. Arthurs, his chauffeur, opened the rear door of the car, a black Armstrong-Siddeley, which was parked by the kerb but he waved him away, explaining that he would walk to his Club and that he, the chauffeur, should pick him up from there at eight o'clock.

'The exercise will do me good,' he said and then added privately to himself, 'Damn clergy, all the bloody same.'

Arthurs, a surly look on his weasel face, watched his employer stride away until he disappeared into Victoria Street. Then he closed the door, lit a cigarette and leaned nonchalantly against the bonnet of the car.

Courtney-Allyn was a troubled man. As he strode towards his Club, he weighed the various points of view in his mind and came to the conclusion that, whether or not the Dean and his "people" were on board, he and his "people" would go ahead with their plan regardless. He had arranged the meeting some time before, surmising that his time with the Dean might prove fruitless. He was on firmer ground now with like-minded people who understood the importance and goals of their enterprise, and as he turned off Victoria Street and took to the narrower roads that led to the rear of the Palace, his mood lightened. He was secure amongst his own, the familiar sites and buildings and the class of people therein that denoted the history and traditions that had stood for nearly two thousand years. By the time he stepped into the vestibule of his Club in Montrose Place, he was positively brimming with hubris.

They had taken a private room — wood-panelled, leather chairs, a comforting fire — and after a round of brandy and cigars, Courtney-Allyn dismissed the waiter and told him that they were, under no circumstances, to be disturbed. Sitting on his right was Viscount Barton, his oldest friend — they had schooled at Eton together — who was almost the exact likeness to the portrait which hung over the fireplace, of his grandfather, the founder of the Club. 'Teddy' Barton was a tall, lean bachelor with a military bearing — he was a Lieutenant Colonel in the Life Guards — and a shock of silver hair which gave him an arresting appearance, a distinction which, over the years, various society ladies had found irresistible. The three others in attendance were all Peers of the Realm: the Earl of Lanchester, a wheezy old ex-cabinet minister; the Duke of Hardwick, who played for the Gentlemen at Lords and was in property, and Bishop Creel, diffident, indecisive, but loyal to the cause. Courtney-Allyn had been unhappy about the inclusion of a member of the clergy but the others had insisted on the grounds that whatever course their mission took it was better to have some inside connection with the Lords Spiritual.

'He's one of us,' Barton had assured him.

For over an hour, their discussion was marked by very little dissent — the Bishop offered an equivocal point of view on various points — and a general willingness to proceed come what may.

'Then we are agreed, gentlemen?' Courtney-Allyn said at

last with some relief as he sat back in his chair.

'I suppose it's too late to…'

'Too late. Preparations already under way,' Barton interrupted the Bishop in his clipped way of speaking, a manner he had cultivated while a cadet at Sandhurst.

Courtney-Allyn pressed home the point. 'Imagine, Your Lordship, if future generations were to learn that we did nothing to protect the sanctity of our class, our way of life?'

Bishop Creel couldn't imagine what it was like to have children but he understood the tenor of his fellow Peer's argument and decided to say no more.

'And England, and everything it stands for. Good God man!' Hardwick added in his blustery fashion.

The Bishop blanched at the mention of his employer and Hardwick, realising his blasphemy, mumbled an apology. Lanchester leaned forward and in a conspiratorial manner said in his high-pitched voice, 'What happens, gentlemen, about the King? When do we…?'

Courtney-Allyn answered emphatically. 'We don't. We should console ourselves with the knowledge that, in certain quarters, the matter is understood, if not spelt out. No one outside of this room, and a few carefully chosen lackeys, will be a party to our plans.' He stood up, faced the others, the light from the fire illuminating his impassioned features. 'In the King's heart of hearts, and in the heart of every English gentleman is the knowledge that what we do, we do for the very soul of our country.'

They raised their brandy glasses, toasted the King and his realm and the meeting came to an end.

Chapter 2

It was late afternoon. The countryside around Compiegne was dull beneath the rain-filled clouds. The black car drove along the country road then turned towards a small chapel that appeared dimly under the trees. The ambulance followed; a large red cross emblazoned on its side. The rain that threatened began just as the car came to a halt under the trees to the side of the chapel. The ambulance drove on, around the side of the building and stopped near the door to the vestry.

Responding to a tap on the glass, the chauffeur slid the dividing glass panel back.

'The other party should be here soon, Arthurs,' Brigadier Courtney-Allyn said. 'Keep your eyes and ears open.'

Arthurs tapped his cap by way of acknowledgement and closed the panel.

'What time do you have, Barton?'

'Just after four,' replied Lieutenant Colonel Barton.

'I hope they won't be late,' said Courtney-Allyn.

They waited. The rain drummed down on the roof. 'Filthy weather, filthy country,' observed the Baron.

The panel slid back again. 'Someone arriving, sir.'

They looked out as a regular army lorry pulled up a few yards away. A burly Sergeant Major climbed out of the cab, walked to the rear and lifted the tarpaulin flap. Two soldiers jumped out, released the tail gate, slid out a plain deal coffin, and with the Sergeant Major leading the way, carried it in through the front door of the chapel. A few moments later they emerged; the two soldiers returned to the lorry and Perry made his way over to the car. The rear window was wound down.

'All correct, sir,' said Sergeant Major Perry and he saluted the occupants.

'Very good, Perry,' said Courtney-Allyn. Then as an afterthought, 'You didn't forget the flag?'

'No, sir. Draped as ordered.' The window wound up. Perry retired to the cab of the lorry. The rain continued lashing down.

Courtney-Allyn sat back, an anxious look on his face. Barton recognised the stress his companion was under and by way of reassurance said, 'Don't worry, Rupert. We're doing the right thing.'

'It's not that,' he snapped back, 'it's having to rely on others...' And he suddenly left his seat, opened the door, and despite the rain, strode purposefully towards the chapel.

Inside, he shook the water droplets from his greatcoat, approached the coffin and lifted a corner of the tattered, war-torn Union Jack. An old rhyme from his childhood, often told by his nanny at bedtime, came to him, 'Tinker, Tailor, Soldier, Sailor, Gentleman, Apothecary...' He hesitated. *Who came next? Ah, yes...* 'Ploughboy... Thief'. For the briefest of moments an expression of sorrow appeared on his face. Then, ashamed of his show of weakness he reasserted the military self-discipline that was his true nature. Barton was right. The stakes were too high for any chances to be taken.

Back in the car, Courtney-Allyn checked his pocket watch.

'They're late,' he muttered.

'They'll be here,' Barton said.

The glass panel slid back. 'Lorries, sir.'

The two military men looked through the rain-splashed

window. Three army trucks turned off the lane and stopped in front of the chapel. Sergeant Major Perry appeared and took charge of the group of soldiers who climbed out of the backs of the trucks and carried three more plain deal coffins into the building. From the efforts of the carriers it was clear that they were not empty. They emerged a minute later and Perry ordered them back into their vehicles.

Arthurs opened the rear door of the car for Brigadier Courtney-Allyn and Lieutenant Colonel Barton and they walked quickly over to the two officers and the Army Chaplain who had gathered outside the chapel.

'Brigadier, Lieutenant Colonel.' Captain Stokes saluted his superiors. 'A filthy day for it.'

'Indeed,' replied Barton.

'Shall we get on,' said Courtney-Allyn. The Chaplain held up his hand.

'Because of the solemn nature of the occasion I feel a few words from the Good Book before...?'

Courtney-Allyn, forever impatient with the clergy, barked out, 'With the greatest respect Your Reverence, there isn't time. Don't forget we have a boat and a train to catch.'

Captain Stokes added, 'If you would care to say a prayer while the ceremony takes place?'

The Chaplain, unhappy with the suggestion but suitably rebuked, nodded his head in agreement and opening his small Bible began to read aloud, 'My father's house has many rooms...'

'I believe you have the... honour, if that is the right word, Lieutenant Colonel?' The Captain addressed Barton.

'Thank you, Captain.'

Barton and Courtney-Allyn exchanged brief conspiratorial

looks and the Lieutenant Colonel stepped inside the chapel. Sergeant Major Perry closed the door behind him and stood as if on guard.

The rain became heavier, drowning out the Chaplain's homily as well as soaking his Bible and he said 'Amen' and dashed back to the truck that had brought him.

Barton emerged, a rather sheepish look on his face, and said, 'It's done. The flag designates the one, Sergeant Major.'

Perry saluted and remained guarding the door.

'Well, gentlemen, shall we get out of the rain?' Captain Stokes suggested and the various parties withdrew. With the field clear, Perry ordered the pallbearers out of their respective trucks, three plain deal coffins were carried back out of the chapel, loaded back onto the vehicles and were driven away. With them out of sight, he marched over to his lorry and ordered his two volunteers to 'follow me.' They went past the black car and around to the side of the building where an ambulance was parked. Arthurs, the chauffeur, joined them. Perry flung open the rear doors of the ambulance to reveal a highly polished oak casket.

'Right, get it out,' Perry yelled and the three volunteers dragged the object out. It was heavy and they struggled to carry it as far as the vestry door, which Perry held open for them. With much manoeuvring, they managed the casket through the narrow doorway and inside and through to the apse. The four trestle tables were still there, but empty. The plain deal coffin draped with the flag, which they had carried in earlier, was still resting on its bier.

'Here,' barked Perry, and he pointed to the table next to the coffin. Perry was forced to lend a hand and deposit the weighty casket in place.

'All right, back to the lorry,' he said.

Outside, the rain was still pouring down.

Perry and the chauffeur hurried over to the black car. 'All correct, sir,' Perry conveyed to Courtney-Allyn and Barton through the wound-down window.

'Good work, Sergeant Ma...' the Brigadier stopped suddenly. He was looking past Perry, at one of the pallbearers who was staring at them intently.

Perry turned and angrily shouted out, 'Get back to the lorry, Burne or I'll have you on a charge!' The soldier called Burne turned away and joined his fellow soldier in the back of the lorry.

'Sorry about that, sir. Bloody troublemaker. He's up before a firing squad in the morning.'

'Good. But... better that he doesn't take any part from here.'

'We'll need an extra pair of hands, sir. The casket is heavy enough without a body in it. What about the ambulance driver?' suggested Perry.

'The less he knows the better.'

'Then I'll get my driver to help us in his place.' He dashed over to the lorry.

Courtney-Allyn turned to Barton. 'You'll forgive me if I stay here in the car while you...'

'I understand entirely. Leave it to me.'

Perry returned with a grumpy looking Groves and a sleepy looking Shippey in tow, and together with Arthurs, followed Barton into the chapel.

Brigadier Courtney-Allyn watched them through the rain- streaked window. He thought of England, of Hopeswell Hall, of how he disliked France and all its associations with the war. He had seen little combat action, having been stationed at company headquarters in a commandeered fourteenth-century

94

chateau well behind the lines. He thought of the time he visited his son at a forwarding station near Arras. He recalled the devastation and the casualties and how he had contrived to get Second Lieutenant Raymond Courtney-Allyn transferred to a safer location away from the killing but even with the connections he had, his efforts were fruitless. His son's desire to serve "God, King and Country" combined with his appetite for glory and adventure proved too strong, and so he had led his men valiantly and died in the process. But it wasn't going to be all in vain, he promised the boy's mother just before she passed away with grief. Their son's memorial would outlive any hopes and dreams that they had ever contemplated for his future...

The vestry door opened and the four pallbearers emerged with the casket, struggling under its weight and slipping on the wet, muddy ground. Barton led the way to the ambulance and once the cargo was safely on board and the rear doors secured he returned to the car.

'Thank you, my friend,' muttered Courtney-Allyn. 'I feel that our plan has legitimacy, now.'

'Of course, it does,' replied Barton. 'Always did have.'

Perry, Groves and Shippey dashed back to the shelter of their vehicle.

Arthurs took his place in the driving seat and slid back the glass panel.

'Ready to move, sir,' he announced.

Barton leaned forward. 'Thank you, Arthurs. We'll just see the burial party off and away...' and he turned his gaze on the lorry. Instead of a plume of exhaust fumes, Perry appeared at a gallop, his face flustered. Barton wound down the window.

'That bloody...'

'What is it?'

'Burne. The bastard. Sorry, Sir. He's scarpered!' He struggled for breath. Courtney-Allyn was struck dumb. Then a look of panic crossed his face.

Barton poked his head out of the car. 'Get after him, man, he can't have gone far!'

'But... in which direction?' spluttered Perry. Barton leapt out of the car. 'Get your men. Search party.'

Perry ran back to the lorry.

'Arthurs, follow me,' bellowed Barton, 'and get the ambulance driver to help.' But after half an hour they returned, sodden and exhausted. Courtney-Allyn had remained behind in the car, his mind befuddled, angry and despairing in turn. Were all of his plans to be put in jeopardy because of one renegade soldier?

Barton climbed in beside him. 'Better get a move on. No time to change plans if we're going to catch that boat.' He rapped his hand on the glass. 'Get a move on, Arthurs.'

The car moved forward, passed the ambulance and headed off down the muddy track away from the chapel and onto the narrow lane. The ambulance fell in behind. 'Don't worry, they'll catch him. He doesn't have a chance,' said Barton reassuringly.

Sergeant Major Perry watched them go, an anxious expression on his ruddy face. 'All right for you. Bloody brass hats!' He stumbled across to the lorry and lifted the flap. Groves was sitting there, a stupid grin on his face.

'I tried to talk him out of it.'

'Like heck you did.' And he threw down the flap and returned to the cab. The lorry pulled away.

'Good luck to him, I says,' Groves muttered, wishing that he'd had the courage to get away.

Perry barked at Shippey and told him to drive back to camp as quickly as possible.

I'm for it now, he thought. *No more perks for me. No leave, no pub, latrine duty if I'm lucky... unless he's caught.*

Chapter 3

A few days later, back at Hopeswell Hall the country seat of the Courtney-Allyns in Huntingdonshire, the Baron studied the newspapers for any reports of the deserter. Each morning he had sent his son Roland down to the village to buy a copy of every paper that came in on the morning train. Each day that passed with no news of a capture increased his sense of anxiety. Viscount Barton had also travelled up, partly to reassure his old friend and partly to get away from his club and the small talk that rumbled around following the ceremony.

'But Teddy, what about the other members of the burial party?' he asked Barton, an uneasy tremble in his voice. They were taking a late breakfast in the morning room.

'I'll see to them, Rupert. We must stick to the plan. I'm returning to London tomorrow and I'll set the wheels in motion.'

'Remind me who there was?'

'Sergeant Major Perry. Groves, the lad who was up for striking his superior officer. Then their driver, I can't recall his name but we'll have to think of something for him. And the ambulance driver, but I don't think we need worry about his part. He was on official duty and was following orders. And Arthurs, of course.'

'Won't this lad, Groves, be shot? It's a capital offence, striking a superior.'

'He's underage. Lied to join up, so it's possible that leniency will be shown.'

'And what did we propose for them?'

'For Perry, when he leaves the service, his own public house in the East End of London, close to where he lives.'

'Bit much isn't it?'

'Don't forget, Rupert, he's the one member of the party we had to divulge certain details to.'

Courtney-Allyn's troubled expression deepened.

'But don't worry. He's a rather dull fellow. It's highly unlikely that he'll put two and two together.'

'And Groves? Have you any influence with the officers heading his court martial?'

'None. It's taking place in France, at the prison camp where he and Burne were serving their sentences.'

'Burne?'

'The escaped man.' Barton gave his friend a concerned look and placed his hand on the Baron's shoulder. 'Try and get some rest, Rupert. These past few weeks have been a trying time... for us all.'

'I'm all right.' He stood up. 'Where's that son of mine? He should have been back with the newspapers by now.'

'You sent Roberts out this morning, Rupert. Don't you recall? Roland didn't come home last night.'

'Oh, yes,' he said vaguely. 'Perhaps you're right, Teddy. Maybe I do need a rest.' He wandered towards the door, then suddenly turned around and regained his military bearing. 'Better make sure of things, Barton, we don't want inquisitive minds coming to any unsavoury conclusions.' And with that, he strutted away.

Barton watched his old friend go with a sense of unease and foreboding. He had worried about his state of mind ever since the death of his son. And the subsequent events in France and the escape of Private Edward Burne had only exacerbated the problem.

On their return to England, the Lieutenant Colonel had moved swiftly into action. Through a fellow peer who had served on a crime commission, he was given the name of a contact at Scotland Yard and from him he had acquired the name of a reliable retired detective who agreed to find out what he could about the missing man.

He didn't go into details with Rupert, just said that 'investigations were ongoing and the entire justice system was on the case.' Although the best of friends, he and the Baron were very different people. He was pragmatic, sociable and decisive in contrast to Rupert who was erratic, remote and often volatile. In fact, this whole affair was the only time he had known the Baron to commit and sustain his attention on something for any length of time. He recalled the day, at their club, when Rupert had burst in to the library and taken him aside. His face was fired with indignation as he reported on the conversation he had just had with a colleague, '…and they are proposing that this… fellow be dug up and buried amongst kings… I mean, Teddy, it could be anyone… a criminal type, a bolshie, a fellow from the working classes…' And since that day the Baron's sole purpose and all of his efforts had been dictated by what he termed 'all that is right and proper.' Despite their differences they had stuck together in the enterprise, not only out of loyalty, but with a sense of the rightness and unquenchable belief in their mission.

In quite a short time, the detective had unearthed certain information from the central Army Records Office, which took him to a church in Holborn that operated a soup kitchen for down-and-outs. Further enquiries led to a woman named Edith Perkins who lived in North West London. Her husband,

Lieutenant William Perkins, had been reported missing in action believed killed, but according to the neighbours, had suddenly returned.

Barton had carried out some ferreting of his own and knew that the deserter was no regular soldier, that Burne had been deemed "officer material" but refused to toe the line and had been reduced to ranks. Further investigation revealed that Burne was self-educated and had trained as an engineer but his 'bolshie' attitude led to him being relieved of his employment. A troublemaker, a rebel, someone too dangerous to be left on the loose and free to come to any awkward deductions.

After his breakfast conversation with Teddy, the Baron retired to his study and lay down on the leather chesterfield that occupied the centre of the room. He reflected with some pride on his efforts over the past days and weeks. Oh yes, others had been involved, especially his friend Teddy Barton, but the original idea, the basic plan, had been his. And then, the culmination...

It had been a suitably solemn affair, and despite the drizzly weather, was attended by thousands of people, who lined the streets in silent deference. A military band led the way down Whitehall followed by columns of soldiers. At the Cenotaph, the King laid a wreath and then walked behind the gun carriage which bore the oak casket into the Abbey. Lieutenant Colonel Barton had accompanied the main party. Brigadier Courtney-Allyn kept a lower profile and stood off to the side amongst one of the groups of military men and clergy. Alongside him stood Bishop Creel, but he studiously avoided any eye contact with the cleric. The hymns and prayers that accompanied the interment passed over him, the procession of royals and politicians paying homage were a blur. He had peace of mind knowing what others didn't but would have wished for, that a member of their class was being entombed amongst their own.

At the conclusion of the ceremony, he had retired to his club with Teddy Barton and recovered with a large glass of malt whisky and eventually had fallen asleep in a large leather chair in front of a blazing fire. Later, in the early evening, when the Abbey had emptied of mourners and sightseers, he paid his own silent homage, careful that the tears that welled up were not noticed by the four sentries guarding the tomb. Afterwards, he wandered along the nave and gazed at the tombs of Kings and Queens, Princes and Knights of the Realm and he took comfort and pride in knowing that his son was in such company. It didn't matter that only a handful knew. What mattered was that the tradition of superior order and class that had made England the nation it was had been maintained for future generations.

He came to the place known as Poet's Corner and his lofty mood changed. He'd never been fond of poetry; indeed, he'd never really understood it. He looked up at a plaque commemorating George Frederic Handel.

'German wasn't he?' He sniffed. He glanced around at the other names. 'I suppose,' he mused, 'there has to be a place for their memory… but here, among the blood royal?' He moved on. He came to a floor stone memorial bearing the name of Charles Darwin and a look of astonishment crossed his face. 'That atheist… He's in here, too?'

The Baron came out of his reverie, a look of disquiet on his face. He sat up. The leather beneath him squeaked.

'It only takes one,' he muttered. 'One malcontent, one dissenter to upset the whole bloody apple cart!'

It was later that day that Roberts apprehended a trespasser prying around in the vicinity of the family burial site.

'Poachers usually stay in the woods, out of sight,' was his challenge to the man, who made no attempt to flee, just gazed at the gamekeeper, an insolent look on his face. Roberts challenged him again and after an explanation the like of which he had heard quite a few times before, he shunted the interloper towards the house and down into the cellar. Not wishing to disturb the Baron, Roberts informed Viscount Barton of his 'find'. On inspection of the man's belongings it didn't take long for suspicions to be aroused and Teddy Barton made a telephone call to London.

Armed with more information, the Baron, his son Rollo and the Viscount confronted the intruder.

PART THREE

Chapter 1

That intruder was me. The interrogation over, I was returned to
my basement cell. It was night again. The Baron's telling had
lasted most of the day. As I sat in the darkness I reflected on
things as they stood. His account had surprised me in its
frankness and detail, as if he had wanted to confirm to himself
the audacity of the venture. Or, perhaps, I thought, he was
motivated by a sense of guilt. But no. I quickly rejected those
ideas. This was no fanatic glorying in his triumph, no zealot
bragging about his cleverness in outwitting others. What was
clear to me was the absolute conviction and resolution of the
rightness of the plan. That line of Macauley's popped into my
head: "The measure of a man's character is what he would do if
he knew he would never be found out." Order and tradition had
been maintained. England would be perpetuated in a state of
unchanging sleep.

Not for the first time I considered my impossible situation.
Every detail of the plot, as related by the Baron, condemned me.
It wasn't a question of knowing too much. I knew everything.
They couldn't let me go now. And if, by some unexpected turn of
events, I was to escape, who would I go to? Who would believe
a deserter, a fugitive? The police? The newspapers, always
hungry for salacious titbits? No, Edward Burne was for it. Well,
I had evaded the firing squad once, and perhaps...

In my innocence I had asked the Baron what had become of
the others that day. Such details were beneath him and so his son

Rollo explained.

'Perry died, kidney failure, I believe.'

'Oh, I heard he was run over by a car,' I cut in. He ignored my outburst.

'Young Groves works for us. Very reliable.'

'You mean he knows his place?'

'Can't recall what happened to the other chap, the driver.'

'Heart attack.' Barton reminded him.

'How very convenient,' I replied in as sarcastic a tone as I could muster and I scanned their smug, self-justified faces hoping for a glimmer of humanity but they just carried on, secure in the knowledge that they, and their kind, were immutable. Like a drowning man clutching at a clump of grass on the riverbank, and in a last desperate attempt to lessen my sentence, I tried to explain that whoever was lying in that tomb in Westminster Abbey meant nothing to me. It was only a symbolic gesture and most people would believe that the body could be one of their own, an uncle, a brother, a father, a husband, and therefore, in a way, they had failed in their venture. It was the only time I noticed a flicker of anger behind the eyes of the Baron but he quickly regained his outward calm. 'You are entitled to be as angry as you wish, Private Edward Burne. Your opinions of our actions are of no concern to us,' he said, a hint of finality in his voice.

My feelings of indignation and injustice counted for nothing. It hadn't been my intention to act as a crusading righter of wrongs. I had only been concerned with finding out what happened that day in France. I recalled my prophecy of the night before last, '...shot in the woods whilst evading capture, a dead rabbit in his pocket...' The local magistrate, Baron Courtney-Allen, presiding passing a verdict of 'death by misadventure' and the case would be closed. I mused over who would fire the gun.

Probably the gamekeeper but then, the surviving son, Rollo, seemed a more likely contender.

'What about your conscience? You'll all have to live with this for the rest of your lives,' I blurted out at them before I was led away.

There was a stony silence and then the Baron spoke. 'Conscience?' He said the word as if it was a dirty word. 'What we did was for God, King and Country. There is no higher calling.'

The basement room was now my death cell. I went to the small ground level window and peered out. It had started to rain. A spark of an idea suddenly came to me. I had escaped once and maybe, if luck was on my side, I could escape again. It would be gloomy in the early morning; they would almost certainly take me to a wooded area... my mind began feverishly to hatch a plan. The darkness and the rain would only aid me and hinder them. But what about Edith? My hopes faded as quickly as they had risen. I couldn't leave her after all she had done for me. Was she due the same fate as me, I asked myself? My captors, I had come to realise, were ruthless despite their detached, passionless English manner. I slumped down on to the hard dirt floor. After all, I reminded myself, I was English too. Why didn't I bear the same characteristics as them? I had stood up to my knees in cold, wet mud for God, King and Country, seen fellow soldiers die horribly, watched as others begged to be shot to end the vicious pain that coursed through their broken bodies; how was I any different? But I knew that, to them, I might have been a visitor from a distant continent.

PART FOUR

Chapter 1

Edith had found the note on the kitchen table, propped up against the tea pot. She read it with trepidation. William had mentioned that he was going away for a few days to 'look up an old army colleague' and he had mentioned that 'something had happened...' Why couldn't he tell her, she asked herself? His sudden absence gave her the dreadful feeling that, this time, he really wouldn't return. Although, she reminded herself, when he had gone before to get in touch with fellow soldiers, he had always come back. She quickly climbed the stairs and found that his uniform was still hanging in the wardrobe. Her suspicions increased; what else was he not telling her? She returned to the kitchen and looked in her purse. A ten-shilling note that she was going to pay the butcher with was missing. She looked in the jam jar that contained any loose change and noticed that it was considerably lower in content.

'Of course,' she convinced herself, 'he needed money for the train and possibly an overnight stay in a hotel.' He had touched upon both possibilities to her a few days ago. 'But why did he not say anything last night,' she deliberated, 'and why the sudden and furtive departure?'

She spent the day fretting, alternately sobbing into her handkerchief and staring, red-eyed, out of the front bay window. As darkness descended, a terrifying thought entered her mind. What if he wasn't "her William" after all? Her anxiety increased as night fell and it wasn't until dawn streaked the sky that she drifted into a troubled sleep, fully clothed, on the couch.

She was awakened early the next morning by a knock at the front door. She opened it still wearing the clothes she had worn the day before, rather crumpled, her hair untidy. She rushed into the hall, her mind in a panic, 'he's forgotten his key...'

She was confronted by two uniformed policemen. Her immediate thought was of William, something had happened to him, an accident... but they reassured her that everything was all right and if she would accompany them to the police station she could help with their enquiries. She wanted to change into fresh clothes but was assured that there was no need as the matter wouldn't take long and she would soon be back home. Her mind was in turmoil. *What could it be? If he was not injured in any way, then...* The awful notion from the night before, that William was not who he said he was, she had banished from her mind.

A car drove Edith and the two policemen away. At the local police station she was shown into a small room with a chair and table lit by a bare bulb hanging from the ceiling. A mug of tea and a plate of biscuits were brought in by a young policeman and she was then left alone for what seemed an eternity.

The door opening noisily brought her out of a trance-like state that had overcome her. The young policeman was accompanied by a man in plain-clothes, wearing a trench coat and hat, who ushered her, gently but firmly, out of the room. It was dark outside; a large car waited at the foot of the steps and the plain-clothes man held open the rear door. As Edith, bewildered and frightened, was helped in she noticed a shield, a crest painted on the door but the form was indistinct, a black bird, perhaps...

The plain-clothes man sat up front next to the driver and they set off. A glass panel separated Edith from them. On the seat was a travelling blanket and a small valise that seemed familiar. Inside was a selection of her clothes, a pair of shoes and a few toiletries. She leaned forward and tapped on the glass. The plain-clothes man slid the panel back. In a tremulous voice, Edith asked him to explain to her what was happening and where they were going. His only response was to half-turn and pass over a pack of sandwiches and a flask of tea after which the panel was firmly closed. Not hungry but weary and frustrated she stared out of the car window. The few street-lit areas soon disappeared and the dark shapes of hedgerows and trees sped by. Eventually, she closed her eyes and slept.

When Edith came to, the car was moving along a gravel drive. She sat up and in the early morning light could see wide expanses of grassland dotted with trees. After a while rhododendron bushes hid that view, and looking through the windscreen, between her two "kidnappers" — for that was who she thought they must be — she saw a large country house appear. As soon as the car stopped, she was hustled out of the back seat by the plain-clothes man and taken around the side of the house, along a path, through a back door and into a small room, not unlike the one at the police station. It also had a rough wooden table and chairs, but there were windows. Her valise, the uneaten sandwiches and flask were brought in by the driver, a thin man with a weaselly face, and placed on the table. She heard the car drive away and was left alone. It was very quiet; the only sound was the chirping of birds from outside. Edith looked out of the window at the land that stretched away to a lake and trees beyond. She wasn't frightened any more. Indeed, how could any harm come to her in such a place? Convinced that soon she would be reunited with William, she sat down and took a bite from one of the sandwiches.

Footsteps, metal on stone, approached. The door swung open and the plain-clothes man entered. With him were two others. A swarthy man in rustic clothes carrying a shotgun and a younger man, wearing evening clothes and a bow tie and looking as if he had just woken up.

Edith put down the half-eaten sandwich.

'Where is William? Where is my husband?'

The plain-clothes man sat down opposite her. 'Do you know a man named Edward Burne?'

Edith stared at him blankly then shook her head.

'He sometimes calls himself William Perkins.'

Edith experienced a sudden rush of excitement which was followed quickly by a feeling of incomprehension. 'I don't understand,' she stammered.

'It's quite simple,' said the younger man. 'The man who says he is your husband, isn't. He's a deserter, a wanted man, a dangerous man.'

Edith stared at him in disbelief. Tears welled up and she shook her head, put her hands over her ears. 'It's not true,' she stuttered through her sobs.

'Do you know where we can find him?'

After an hour of further questioning the plain-clothes detective and Rollo left her with Roberts.

Outside the sun was trying to come out from behind the clouds.

Rollo lit a cigarette.

'We'll get no more from her. Not in the state she's in,' said the detective.

'Seems off her head to me.'

'You can tell your father that I think she knows nothing more than she has told us.'

'Or not told us.'

'What will you do with her?'

'That's up to my father. He's the local magistrate.'

The plain-clothes detective shuffled his feet uneasily. He had been hired to find the deserter Burne and had, instead, only come up with a woman who might, or might not, be his wife.

'I shall carry on with my search, then.'

'That won't be necessary,' came the abrupt reply and Rollo turned and slouched back towards the house. 'Send your bill in, we are no longer in need of your services,' he called out before disappearing.

The plain-clothes detective returned to London by train that same day. As he stared out at the countryside dashing by he wondered what it had all been about. He wondered whether or not he ought to take the matter up with the senior officer who had contacted him in the first place. But he thought better of it. "A case that requires your utmost discretion," was how it had been put to him. He sat back, closed his eyes and slept until the train terminated at St Pancras station two hours later.

He was at his desk, a few days after the affair, when an item in the newspaper caught his attention.

"*Private Edward Burne, wanted by the military police for desertion, was shot in the early hours of yesterday morning whilst attempting to evade capture. His presence in the grounds of Hopeswell Hall, was a mystery but it was thought that he was attempting to return to his childhood home in Lincolnshire. The gamekeeper, Gabriel Roberts, told the inquest how he had been losing game from traps set out around the estate. When he had surprised a man in the act of stealing from one of his traps, he had challenged him but the poacher had run away and he was obliged to loose off both barrels. Two dead rabbits were found on the dead man's person. No blame was attached to Roberts who has been a loyal and diligent servant for over twenty years. The inquest, chaired by local magistrate, Baron Courtney-Allyn, passed a verdict of death by misadventure, but added, '...in light of Private Burne having escaped prior to his having to face the firing squad for desertion, the court feels that justice has been served.'"*

The plain-clothes man looked up and recalled his recent dealings with the Courtney-Allyn family.

Rather a coincidence that this chap, Burne, should turn up a few days after I had questioned that woman, he thought. *What was her name...?* But it wouldn't come to mind and he turned the page and switched his attention to the financial column and the latest price on a small investment he had recently placed on the stock market exchange.

PART FIVE

Chapter 1

During the 1960s, a move was made by various local authorities to reform institutional care. Many old, large Victorian buildings were deemed no longer desirable, or affordable, for the incarceration of the sick and mentally ill. One such institution in Lincolnshire, Brackenbury Hall, was thus earmarked for closure and the occupants relocated. The last to be moved was a 68-year-old woman who had spent almost all of her adult life in care.

On the morning of the day she was to be transferred to a new care facility, she listened as a young doctor from the district health foundation attempted to explain the reasons behind her transfer, but she didn't seem to fully comprehend what he was saying. She was all ready to go; the nurse had arrived earlier and dressed her, and after a quick breakfast, she sat on the chair by the barred window, her overcoat on, waiting patiently for... for what, she wondered?

The doctor glanced down at her file. 'No health issues to speak of, just that which comes to us all,' he half-joked. 'How long has Miss Perkins been here?'

'As long as I have, Doctor, and then some, I believe,' the nurse replied.

He stared down at the frail, withdrawn creature and was surprised when a glimmer of compassion came to him. He consulted the notes in her file.

'Committed in 1920,' he muttered. 'Was found abandoned and suffering from loss of memory. The local magistrate, the

Right Honourable Rupert Courtney-Allyn presiding, had her committed to a series of institutions, the last being Brackenbury Hall. No next of kin or relatives could be found, so...' He turned the page. 'Oh!'

'What's that, Doctor?' asked the nurse.

'This Courtney-Allyn was on the board here... until he died in 1946. Then his son, Roland, took over.'

The nurse seemed unconcerned. She pulled open a drawer and began to place the old woman's clothes neatly in a suitcase. 'The local gentry over at Hopeswell Hall. My sister-in-law used to clean for them. But... Do all sorts of charity work. He opened the summer fete.'

The doctor continued reading. 'It seems a special injunction was granted Miss Perkins. "Never to be discharged..." Signed by both Courtney-Allyns. And now she's to be sent to Bridgemoor. But that's an asylum.'

Mystified, he gazed down again at the old woman.

'She hasn't been any trouble, has she? You know, violent or...?'

'No. No trouble. Anyhow, not since I've been working here.'

'And this report says, she's never had visitors?'

'If that's what it says, Doctor.'

'Strange...' he murmured to himself.

The old woman looked up at him, inclined her head slightly as if in recognition of something and held out her bony hand. 'William...' Her voice was thin and weak.

'What? What did you say?' The doctor leaned closer and she repeated the name. He straightened up and turned to the nurse. 'Who is William?'

The nurse let out a derisory laugh, shrugged and finished sorting out the old woman's clothes.

'Not much to show for all her time here,' said the doctor as he peered into the half-empty suitcase. The nurse replied by snapping it shut.

The doctor hesitated for a moment, as if caught in an irregularity not allowed for by seven years at medical school.

'Well, I've done what I can for... Miss Edith Perkins.' He closed the file and walked out.

An hour later, Edith was sitting in the back seat of a minicab driving away from Brackenbury Hall towards her new home. A male nurse was in the front passenger seat, smoking a cigarette and chatting with the driver.

The sensation of mobility, although rare, was not an altogether unfamiliar one and it brought on a series of recollections from her remote past. Indistinctly at first, then with increasing clarity, she recalled a journey, in a vehicle that was more spacious than this one — the seats were different, black leather not beige plastic, the smell was different — and it was at night, not during the daytime.

As the drive continued, through alien streets, past rows of anonymous houses, she turned her attention to the two men in the front of the minicab and became aware of how they contrasted with her memory of the two who were up front that night. The young driver had worn a dark uniform and had ginger hair. The other, sitting alongside him, was chubby, middle-aged and had scruffy grey hair and bloodshot eyes. She especially recalled his eyes. He had turned in his seat to look at her, not out of any concern, but with a hint of resentment. And then, slowly, came the realisation that the journey had been to the place she had just left and which had been her home for the last... however many years. But there had been another house, a smaller one, on the side of a hill, with a garden, and yes, of course, William. And for a moment, William — he was her husband, seemed to be two people. But she had been alone in the back seat of the larger car. When they had arrived at the home, she recalled dimly, she had been led up the steps and into the grand hall by the middle-aged man. They were met by a nurse with whom he had a brief, but intense, conversation and then he left and she was shown up to a room with a bed and a chair and a chest of drawers and a barred window which became her home for the next... how many years had it been?

An intense feeling of anxiety overwhelmed her until, gradually, the images, spectres in a shadowy journey and a once-lived life, faded away, never to return.

Rollo gazed out of the large picture window and considered the view. As they had driven up the long drive to the house, he had made a mental note that the parkland, once lush and verdant had been neglected. The grass was overgrown and straggly, the trees stunted or fallen; the gravel drive had weeds growing out of it. 'I must have a word with Roberts,' he told himself. Then he remembered that he had left after that shooting incident. 'And the overseer, what was his name? No wonder the place is going to the dogs. There's just no sense of loyalty any more.'

Although Groves had stayed. He had replaced Arthurs, who had succumbed to Spanish flu, as chauffeur to the family. He was cleaning the car over by the outbuildings, his uniform unbuttoned, his ginger hair flopping over his artless, unquestioning face. Rollo noted that the crest on the door was faded almost to obscurity. 'Must get someone to touch it up, display the colours, fly the flag,' he said, but with little conviction.

An hour ago, they had returned from carrying out a

wearisome, but necessary, task. The handover of the woman had gone smoothly; no awkward questions had been asked. She had been a problem for the family for a number of years, shunted around from home to home until, finally, she was committed to Brackenbury Hall. On his father's death, Rollo had succeeded to the board and had, after objections from other board members, anxious as to the woman's origins and the thorny question as to how deranged she actually was, rubber-stamped the move. It was all over.

He collapsed into a leather armchair and poured himself a glass of whisky. It was a cold day; the open fire was unlit. He pulled the plaid blanket from the back of the chair, laid it over his legs and poured himself another drink. He was forty-nine years old but looked much older. His hair was unkempt and grey, his eyes bloodshot; his midriff sagged over skinny legs. He suffered from gout which had kept him out of the last war, much to his relief.

'Too young for the first one, too drunk for the second,' was how his father's old friend, Viscount Barton had succinctly put it.

The 39th Baron Courtney-Allen, the custodian of Hopeswell Hall, had to do his drinking at home having been barred from, not only the village inn, but also his London club. Until recently he had taken to driving out to another county where he was not known and spending the evening imbibing, but the confiscation of his driving licence after a particularly bad accident involving a delivery motorcycle had curtailed that activity. Worse was the incident at Christmastime when he had shot a twelve-year-old boy who had come onto the estate to steal mistletoe and who Rollo, in a drunken haze, had assumed was a poacher. Of course, he'd got away with it; the boy had only suffered superficial wounds, but his shotgun licence was suspended indefinitely. 'Wouldn't have happened if Pa had been on the bench,' he had mused at the time.

He finished the last of the whisky and pulled the chord to summon a servant but no one came and eventually he fell into a befuddled sleep.

Since his father's death the property and surrounding land had indeed fallen into a state of neglect and decay. Over the years, Rollo had frittered away most of the assets at the gaming table. A marriage to a titled lady, for whom he had an intense dislike and who returned the feeling, had been hurriedly arranged. The single aim was to produce a male heir to carry on the succession. But after two weeks she left him and sued for divorce citing mental cruelty. In truth, Rollo wasn't cruel, just stupid and arrogant.

He awoke suddenly from his drunken stupor just as the light was leaving the sky and realised he must have slept for the bulk of the daylight hours. He rang again for a servant but then recalled that it was his day off, or had he fired him for insubordination? He stood up and shuffled over to the mantelpiece, struck a match and lit a candle. The oil painting of a distant ancestor, hanging above him, was illuminated, its features indistinct through the layer of dust and time-worn exposure. A muffled noise, like a footstep, made him turn. He looked across the large oval table in the centre of the room, where, in the gloomy half-light appeared a figure, standing casually, a shotgun under his arm. Another person was in front of him, a younger man, scruffily dressed. And for a moment, his father came into sight, leaning threateningly across the table. Rollo trembled as he seemed to recall an incident from many years ago, after the war, the first one. And as the apparitions glimmered in the half-light, he remembered his brother, Raymond, the chosen son, the gifted one, the athlete, the scholar… and the devastation when the telegram arrived.

He rubbed his eyes, peered into the gloom and the shades disappeared and he was, once again, alone in the cavernous room, in the empty house.

A storm, some days later, brought down a few trees on the grounds of Hopeswell Hall, one of which, a copper beech, crashed through the roof of the family vault. It spared the tombs of the last Baron and his wife but broke the lid of the tomb that was the final resting place of their eldest son, killed in action in 1917.

No one heard the sound of the wood splintering or the stone cracking. However, the early morning light revealed an emptiness. No bones, no decayed winding sheet, just a small amount of dust and debris, as if, after the branches penetrated the stone coffin, the terrible secret that lurked within was, at last, released and could, a free spirit, haunt the empty, wasted land that was England.

THE END